WHERE DO I BELONG?

Something about Mr. Innskeep's words had gotten to that private place inside me. To the me who was adopted. To the me who was unreal.

What's real?

Real is knowing who your parents are. I mean, the ones you came from. Real is knowing who you look like and what you'll look like in the future. Real is growing up with your original mother and father, sisters and brothers, aunts and uncles, grandmothers and grandfathers. Real is having a family tree.

I don't look like anyone on either side of my adoptive family. No one seeing me with them would have thought I belonged there.

The question was: Where did I belong?

I had to find out. Before it was too late.

I'M STILL ME

"In writing this, her first novel, Betty Lifton, an adoptee herself, has drawn meaningfully on her own life experiences and those of other adoptees."

—*Connecticut English Journal*

"The tensions in her narration provide an element of suspense that sustains the reader's interest. . . . The tone of the novel is sincere and its truths are worth sharing."

—*ALAN Review*

D1595789

CARIBOU by Meg Wolitzer
HARRY AND HORTENSE AT HORMONE HIGH
   by Paul Zindel
HOLLYWOOD DREAM MACHINE by Bonnie Zindel
LISTEN CHILDREN by Dorothy S. Strickland
LITTLE LITTLE by M. E. Kerr
ON THAT DARK NIGHT by Carol Beach York
ONLY MY MOUTH IS SMILING by Jocelyn Riley
RILLA OF INGLESIDE (ANNE OF GREEN
   GABLES #8) by L. M. Montgomery
A STAR FOR THE LATECOMER
   by Paul and Bonnie Zindel
TRUE LOVE (CAITLIN #3) by Francine Pascal
ZORRO AND THE PIRATE RAIDERS by D. J. Arneson
ZORRO RIDES AGAIN by D. J. Arneson

I'm Still Me

Betty Jean Lifton

BANTAM BOOKS

TORONTO • NEW YORK • LONDON • SYDNEY • AUCKLAND

RL 5, IL age 11 and up

I'M STILL ME
A Bantam Book / April 1982

PRINTING HISTORY
Alfred A. Knopf edition published April 1981
2nd Bantam printing . .April 1986

ISBN 0-553-25468-5

Published simultaneously in the United States and Canada

Bantam Books are published by Bantam Books, Inc. Its trademark,
consisting of the words "Bantam Books" and the portrayal of a
rooster, is Registered in U.S. Patent and Trademark Office and in
other countries. Marca Registrada. Bantam Books, Inc., 666 Fifth
Avenue, New York, New York 10103.

PRINTED IN THE UNITED STATES OF AMERICA

O   11   10   9   8   7   6   5   4   3   2

For
Karen, Ken, and Bottomless Pit
  and
Stephanie, Susie, and Liz—
  totally!

one

It may sound weird to say that your whole life changed because of an American history assignment. But that's the way it was.

If Mom and Dad had known what was going to happen that day, they would have gone to the principal and demanded a curriculum change. Or that Mr. Innskeep be fired. Or they would have pulled me out of school. Because at that time there were certain things that we just didn't talk about in our house —and one of them was where my younger brother Mike and I come from.

All of which is a way of saying I'm adopted—which until recently I never said at all. It was a secret that I kept in a private place inside me. It didn't bother me because I never thought about it—much. And I might not have thought about it this year if it hadn't been for Mr. Innskeep's history project.

I'm in my junior year at Buckeye High in Southhaven, Connecticut, and I have history the last period on Monday, Wednesday, and Friday. This was Monday, right after Christmas vacation. I had Mr. Innskeep last semester too, so I thought nothing he would do could surprise me anymore. For just as Innskeep is not an ordinary name (he says his family must have been innkeepers in rural England before they migrated here a couple of centuries ago), neither is he an ordinary man. On his desk is a placard that reads:

> Good friend, for Jesus' sake forbear
> To dig the dust enclosed here;

> Blest be the man that spares these stones,
> And curst be he that moves my bones.

Those are the words that William Shakespeare had put on his tombstone. Mr. Innskeep is the head of the Shakespeare Club, and come to think of it, he looks a little like those pictures you see of the Bard. A long thin face, short pointed beard, and piercing dark eyes. His life is just about as mysterious as Shakespeare's too. I mean, we're just not sure of anything about him, like whether he's married or if he lives with anyone.

Once when I called his house at night to ask about an assignment, a man answered the phone and said he was out. But another time when Maggie Brooks (she's my best friend) called, a woman answered. So we don't know what to think.

Anyway, Mr. Innskeep not only teaches history, he lives it. He says that it's only an accident of fate that we were born in this century instead of in the Middle Ages, and that our customs today are influenced by how people lived in the old days.

Everyone agrees that Mr. Innskeep's ideas are sort of weird, but that doesn't keep him from being the most popular teacher at school. He's always thinking of *living* projects (his word) so that we will *feel* history (also his word). Last semester he was into Indians, and we all had to take Indian names, wear beads and blankets, and behave as if we were authentic Indians.

My name was Running Stream. I made up a whole story about her life. Her mother's name was Deep Water and her father was Thunder Cloud. I gave her three sisters: Red Wing, Bright Feather, and Swift Wind. I really like imagining myself as someone else and having other families. It's why I like acting so much. But I had no idea when I was the make-believe Running Stream that in the next history project I was going to become someone real.

You see, I've always felt unreal. In a romantic way, of course. It probably all has to do with my being adopted and not being able to share it with anyone. I didn't want the other kids to think I was different—a freak or something.

Well, there we were that Monday, watching Mr. Innskeep

up at the blackboard, jiggling the chalk from hand to hand the way he always does, and giving us that sly look he gets when he's about to spring something on us.

"This term we're not going to study *other* people," he informed us. "We're going to study *ourselves*." (Pause here as he let this sink in.) "We're going to think of ourselves as *living history*."

Bottomless Pit, who sits across from me, made a gun out of his fingers at this point, put it to his head, blew his brains out, and slumped over his desk. (The boys in our class are really retards. They haven't changed since the eighth grade. Maggie says it's because they mature much later than girls.)

"We're making history right now," Mr. Innskeep was saying, staring at his chalk, which was fairly flying through the air with his words. "Someday, centuries from now, high school kids will study how you dressed, the food you ate, the words you used."

"The four-letter ones too?" asked Bottomless Pit, returned to life, unfortunately as obnoxious as ever. His real name isn't Bottomless Pit, of course, but Jeffrey Branfield. He's fat and awkward because all he does is eat. When his mouth isn't full of smartass cracks, it's full of chocolate bars, which he keeps stashed away in his desk.

"Especially the four-letter words," said Mr. Innskeep, who was used to Bottomless Pit and not particularly bothered by him—especially since he'd done such a great job playing Sitting Bull in our project play just before Christmas. He died gloriously then, delivering his last words with enough expression to bring tears to your eyes even if you remembered who was under all that war paint and feathers.

"The point is," Mr. Innskeep was saying, "how much do you know about your own families? Where they came from?"

"Mine came over on the *Mayflower*," shouted Hortense Hopkins, waving her hand frantically.

Maggie and I exchanged looks across the room. Hortense was really obnoxious on this subject. We'd been hearing about the *Mayflower* since the first grade.

"That's right, Hortense, you do know," Mr. Innskeep continued. "But what about the rest of you? Do you know what ships your great-grandparents, or your grandparents, came over on? Or why they left home? Or what they were like at your age?"

We could tell that Mr. Innskeep was really warming up to the subject the way he was pacing up and down in front of the blackboard.

"For that matter, do you know very much about your own parents? Have you any idea what kind of schools they went to? How they met? Where they lived before you were born?"

He was so excited he almost shouted these last questions at us, and then it all connected. I mean Maggie and I had been really amazed when he assigned a rerun of the TV show "Roots" just before Christmas. In his view, television is a waste of time and will make idiots of us all, if it hasn't already by the time we reach his classroom. But when he discussed "Roots" there was a kind of reverence in his voice. He said it didn't matter that it wasn't great art, or that we weren't all black. He said we could learn a lot from the way the show traced the history of Kunta Kinte's family from their village in Africa, through their slave days, and right up to today.

Now he took a piece of chalk and drew two short vertical lines on the board, and some long ones circling over it, until he had a tree. A few wolf whistles came from the back of the room when he'd finished. It wasn't a great tree. It reminded me of those stenciled trees that were always tacked to our Sunday School bulletin board when I was younger. One quarter would buy a leaf, and when the branches were full, the money went to Israel to plant small forests.

According to Mr. Innskeep, we were to fill in our trees with the names of our parents, their parents, their parents' parents, and so on as far back as we could go.

"A family tree, that's what each and every one of you is going to draw up this semester," Mr. Innskeep said. "Everyone on earth is born to someone and connected by the roots of their tree. We're going to be family explorers and dig up those roots."

As he spoke I got a sick feeling, the way I feel when I've been riding in a car too long. Sort of dizzy, like I need air. I could hear Mr. Innskeep's voice growing fainter and fainter, as if he were on the roof and his words were coming in through the window.

"It won't be easy," he was saying. "Even William Shakespeare" (and he pointed to that placard on his desk) "did not want future generations to dig the dust or move the bones within his grave. It was his way of saying he wanted to leave the mysteries of his life unsolved. And they still are. Even today we know very little about him."

I knew I had to get out the door before it was too late —before I threw up or passed out, or did something equally gross. The last thing I heard was "And so you are going to get busy digging up your family secrets," and then I was in the hall. The walls began tilting and closing in on me.

I guess I'd always known this moment was going to come. And now it was here.

two

I managed to make it to the nurse's office. Fortunately, she was off that afternoon, so I didn't have to explain anything. Unfortunately, there was still half an hour to wait until the bell, so I stretched out on the narrow cot and closed my eyes, hoping that when I opened them the history project would be nothing more than a bad dream.

Maggie and I used to play a game called "Fortunately and Unfortunately." I thought about it now—like Fortunately, I had been adopted by wonderful parents who gave me everything and loved me and had saved me from being brought up in an orphanage; but Unfortunately, I didn't know anything about where I came from and couldn't deal with the subject at all. Something about Mr. Innskeep's words had gotten to that private place inside me. To the me who was adopted. The me who was unreal.

What's real?

Real is knowing who your parents are. I mean, the ones you came from. Real is knowing who you look like and what you'll look like in the future. Real is growing up with your original mother and father, sisters and brothers, aunts and uncles, grandmothers and grandfathers.

Real is having a family tree.

I don't mean to sound ungrateful. I know I do have a tree —my adoptive parents' tree. But it's not the same. I may love Mom and Dad very much, and all my family, but they have nothing to do with me—biologically, that is.

Lying there, I remembered Thanksgiving, when Mom's two

brothers came in from Chicago with their wives and children. They didn't bring my grandfather, because he's been in a nursing home since Gram died three years ago, but they started reminiscing about how he came over from Russia so he wouldn't get conscripted into the czar's army. How he started out with a horse and wagon peddling fruits and vegetables in Chicago, and worked his way up to become a successful textiles manufacturer.

I could see Mom was getting teary while they were talking because she missed having him and Gram there. But I kept thinking that as much as I loved my grandparents, they were not really related to me. I mean by blood. I didn't know anything about my real grandparents.

I glanced around the table at my two uncles, whose hair is almost the same shade of red as Mom's, and at their kids, who have the same hair and the same hazel eyes. Sometimes people say I look like Mom, but my hair is light brown and I have dark eyes. Also, I'm much slimmer than Mom. Sometimes I see mothers and daughters who look exactly alike walking down the street. It gives me a lonely feeling.

Everyone in Dad's family has what they call the Elkins nose —long and broad—and dark hair. At least Dad's was dark until what's left of it starting turning gray a few years ago. His hairline has receded so far back it has no place left to go. You could even say he was bald, except that he has a lot of what he calls "fringe benefits" on each side—long strands which he combs across his forehead as if they're growing there.

I don't look anything like him either. No one seeing me at that table would have thought I belonged there.

The question was: Where did I belong?

The bell rang, bringing me back to my present dilemma. I jumped up quickly and ran to grab my coat from the locker so I wouldn't meet anyone in the halls and have to explain my sudden exit from class. Then I headed for the steps in front of school to meet Maggie.

"Lori Elkins, what's going on?" I heard Maggie's voice rushing ahead of her, the way it always does. "Where'd you disappear to?"

"I'll tell you in the car," I said under my breath as we headed for the parking lot.

Maggie's the only girl in our class who has her own car—a Volkswagen Rabbit. It's really neat. Bright red. Dad says he didn't get a car till he graduated from college, and I don't think I will either.

"So what's the big mystery?" Maggie said when we were out of sight of the school. "Why'd you split?"

"I'm dropping out of history," I replied dramatically. "Unless Mr. Innskeep drops the spring project."

"Give me another clue," she said. "I'm lost."

"I'm not good at drawing trees."

"You don't have to draw anything," she tried to reassure me. "He's giving us mimeographed sheets of family trees that he got free from some genealogical library. All we have to do is fill in the blanks."

"That's the problem. Mine's a total blank."

"Oh, gosh Lori, I'm sorry. I'm really dense."

I'd told her about my adoption two years before when I was sleeping over at her house. We were lying in the dark telling each other our deepest secrets. She told me that her father died when she was a baby and that her mother refused to tell her anything about him. The only father she's ever known is Alan, whom her mother married when she was five. He's a math professor at Southhaven Community College. Maggie really loves him, but that has nothing to do with her wanting to know about her real father.

And then I confessed that I was adopted. Maggie was the only one I'd ever told, except for Sue O'Brian, my former baby-sitter, who lives next door to us.

Maggie was intrigued and full of questions: Couldn't your parents have children of their own? (Which was obvious, because if they could have, they wouldn't have adopted me.) Who are your real parents? Why did they give you away? (As if I knew.)

I explained that my real parents were very poor and couldn't keep me. That I didn't know anything more about them. She said that was too bad, and that seemed to exhaust the subject.

There's not too much to talk about when you don't know anything.

Maggie and I felt very close after that, but we'd never brought up either secret again until now.

"What am I going to do?" I moaned. "How can I admit in front of everyone that I don't have a family tree?"

"Actually, you have *two* trees when you stop to think about it," Maggie said.

"Two?" I pondered this. "A lot of good it does me."

"So just do one."

"Which one?"

"The one you know."

"I only know my adoptive family's. At least some of it."

"Then do that one. You see, it's all very simple."

But, of course, it wasn't that simple. I knew I'd feel like a fraud handing in my adoptive parents' tree, because my parents' ancestors aren't really mine, even though my parents are my parents. It was so hard to explain, even to Maggie. I felt guilty and confused, as if there were some wires crossing in my head that I couldn't straighten out. They kept me from thinking clearly. I didn't want to cry, but now the tears started flooding out.

"That does it," Maggie said, turning in to the Spice Box, one of the drive-ins we pass on the way to my house. "We're both having hot fudge sundaes," she announced to me as well as to the waitress who had bounded over to us on roller skates.

"But your diet," I sobbed, not wanting to feel guilty about Maggie too.

Maggie has a body that inflates and deflates like a balloon. One month she splurges on food until she blows up, and the next month she thins down on the latest fad diet, which means bringing things like carrot sticks and cucumbers to school as lunch.

"Diet, shmiet," she said now. "This is more important. It's therapeutic."

It's not that you can tell Maggie is fat, even when she's off her diet. She likes to wear billowing peasant blouses with skirts almost to her ankles, so she's all hidden most of the time anyway. Even her dark hair, which she wears long and parted in the middle, falls over a good part of her face. But she's really pretty. She has large green eyes that are always full of mischief, and milk-white skin that turns red instead of tanning in the sun.

Anyway, the sundaes helped. We devoured them in silence, and then Maggie pulled out one of the thin cigars she's always filching from her mother, and sat back to light it.

"Maybe your parents will tell you something about your real family tree if you ask," she said, blowing a perfect smoke ring over my head.

"I can't. It would hurt them too much."

"Yeah, I know what you mean," she said softly.

And then I realized that I'd been so concerned with myself that I hadn't even thought about Maggie. Not knowing anything about her real father, I mean.

"What are *you* going to do?" I asked her.

"I don't know," she said, shrugging. "I guess I'll just hang my stepfather on the tree."

She sent another smoke ring sailing over us.

"Anyway, we've got time. The assignment for this week is to interview our grandparents about their lives when they were young. Mr. Innskeep says that a real genealogist works one generation at a time, so that the family continuity isn't lost. But we've got to delve very cleverly so that no family secrets are lost either. He even quoted *Hamlet:* 'There are more things in heaven and earth, Horatio, / Than are dreamt of in your philosophy.' "

She imitated his voice perfectly, and if I hadn't been so miserable, I might have laughed.

We were quiet for some time, watching the rollerskating wonder zoom from car to car.

"You know, speaking of grandparents, I've never met my father's parents," Maggie said, sort of wistfully. "And Lisa's parents won't be back from Florida in time." (Maggie always calls her mother by her first name.) "I don't know what I'm going to do."

Then she started the car, and we sped off as if escaping from it all.

When I got home, I could hear Mom in the den telling Mike to turn off the TV and start his homework. Fortunately, she didn't hear me. Unfortunately, my golden cocker spaniel, Winkie, did. I grabbed him just as he was about to give a welcoming yelp and dashed up the stairs with him into the bathroom I share with Mike.

I locked the door and splashed cold water on my face. My eyes, slightly red and swollen, were waiting for me in the mirror. "You're a mess," they told me.

We were used to looking at each other, my eyes and I. It wasn't vanity on my part, though they are my best feature. I've always wished my face wasn't so round and wholesome, that I had high cheekbones with tragic, sunken hollows under them, like Scarlett O'Hara. Anyway, I was looking for someone whenever I looked into my eyes like this—my real mother or my real father.

Sometimes my eyes looked back at me and said, "Everything's going to be all right." But now they were saying, "You're in trouble. You can't put a pair of eyes on a family tree."

Or can you?

I could see my tree covered with eyes, like the eyes in a peacock's tail. The very idea made me shudder. Peacocks are considered bad luck in the Elkins family. As my father tells it, his father was very ill as a young man with a mysterious ailment. A relative decided that a pair of porcelain peacocks on the mantelpiece was the cause and advised throwing them out. As soon as this was done, my grandfather rose from his bed and was never sick a day in his life after that, until he keeled over from a heart attack when I was ten.

Even though I love birds, I've always been afraid of peacocks. It gives me the creeps to see their long feathers sitting as decorations in someone's home.

"But maybe the peacock is only bad luck for the Elkins family and not your real family," my eyes were telling me now. It was a new thought. Maybe the peacock didn't recognize human arrangements like adoption. . . .

My reverie in front of the mirror was broken by Mike

pounding at the door, and Mom calling from downstairs, "Lori, is that you in the bathroom? I didn't hear you come in."

"Yes," I shouted back, flinging the door open and sweeping past Mike without a word.

"Are you coming down to help me?" she wanted to know.

"Don't count on it," I heard my father say as he walked in the front door.

Dad always says that. He thinks it's funny. I'll say something simple like, "I hope my biology teacher appreciates all the work I've done on this paper," and he'll quip, "Don't count on it."

Mike and I used to tease him about it, and sometimes when he told us to do something, we'd say, "Don't count on it."

But we knew we could always count on *him,* even if he did leave most of the details of raising us to Mom. She's really the boss, but when Dad gets mad and steps in—which isn't often —we really listen. That is, we used to, until Mike stopped listening to anyone this year.

I got through dinner without Mom and Dad noticing anything. Not that they would have anyway, they were so focused on Mike. As usual, he was a mess, with his shirt hanging out of his jeans and dirt streaks on his wrists marking the high-water line above which he made it a point of honor not to wash. His dark brown hair, which was a mass of angelic ringlets when he was younger, now resembled a mop that needed a good shaking out. But then Mike, in general, could have used a good shaking.

The conversation at dinner was the pits.

MOM: You don't have to put everything into your mouth at once, Mike.

MIKE: Leave me alone.

DAD: Eat more slowly, Mike.

MIKE: I'll eat like I want to.

MOM: Did you hear what I said? Don't shovel everything in so fast.

MIKE: Give me a break, will you?

DAD: Don't be rude to your mother, Mike.

MIKE: *(Jumping up and knocking his chair over as he exits from the room)* Get off my case!

Mom and Dad just looked at each other helplessly, and I started clearing the table to stay out of it. I knew they had run out of threats and punishments with him. He'd been impossible almost from the moment he was old enough to understand he could torment them. He kept them so busy with his problems that sometimes they acted as if they had only one child—him. While I, Goody Two-Shoes, could just grow up by myself.

When I finished rinsing the dishes and loading the dishwasher (my job), I raced to my room, got into my pajamas, and crawled into bed. Sleep has always been my escape from the world. I tried to ignore Winkie's scratching at the door—he likes to lie under my desk while I do my homework. But he sleeps in the hall at the top of the steps so he can be in control of all the comings and goings.

"Stop it, Winkie," I hissed.

He took the hint, but then my phone rang, forcing me to sit up and reach for the receiver. I got my own phone line last year because Mom was afraid that she'd never hear from the outside world again if I didn't.

It was Chris—Christopher Barlow. He just transferred to our school from California this year. He's been in and out of schools for various reasons, some of which he talks about and some he doesn't. He says his parents are taking a trip around the world and arranged for him to stay with his aunt and uncle here. He calls Buckeye High boring, but I think he likes it, because he hasn't dropped out yet.

Maggie couldn't believe it when Chris started calling me over Christmas vacation. I couldn't either. If there were a contest for the best-looking guy at our school, I guess he'd win it. He has sleek black hair that he wears long in back—but not too long—and big dark eyes—bedroom eyes, Maggie's mother called them when we dropped by to take Maggie with us to the movies one night. She thought he looked more like an Italian movie star than a high school senior.

Anyway, there he was on the other end of the phone line.

"Hi, Lor." (That's what he calls me.) "Why'd you take off so quickly today?"

"I had to get home, that's all. I really can't talk now, Chris."

"Why? Whatcha doing?"

"Sleeping."

"Sleeping? Want some company?"

"No thanks."

He was always making suggestive remarks like that, but I knew by now he didn't mean them. Maggie was sure he'd try to tear my clothes off the first night we went out, but the truth is that he hardly did anything more than put his arm around me in the car when we parked someplace to listen to music. (Maggie said he must be in remission, and to be on the alert in case he suddenly revved up.)

"I really mean it, Chris, I can't talk. I feel sort of sick. I may be coming down with the flu."

"It's going around," he said. "I'll call tomorrow if you're not in school."

And he hung up quickly, like I might be contagious.

I put the receiver down and the pillow over my head, hoping to close the world out for good.

"Lori, why are you lying there in the dark?"

It was my mother. She has a bad habit of not knocking before opening my door, as if I were still a child waiting to be tucked in.

She sat down on the foot of my bed. Winkie was with her. He scratched at the pillow and his wet nose burrowed against my face.

"Are you feeling all right?" There was concern in her voice. "I'm sorry I was so cross at dinner. Mike flunked another English test today, after I drilled him all last night." It sounded as if she were announcing the latest disaster of Hurricane Someone or Other. Hurricane Mike, that's what he should have been called.

"Bully for him," I muttered from my pillow.

"What did you say, dear?"

"Nothing. I'm sleeping, Mom."

What I felt like saying was that I was sick and tired of having everything revolve around that thirteen-year-old brat. I know it's a difficult age and all that, but sixteen's no picnic either. And there wasn't ever a time when Mike wasn't flunking math or English, in spite of tutors, school psychologists, and Mom sitting with him over his homework all the time. He'd never been good in school like I was. Right from the beginning he'd had trouble learning to read. He couldn't stay still in class. He almost flunked kindergarten, which is a pretty hard thing to do—how can you flunk building blocks? The teacher said he wasn't mature enough to go into first grade. But Dad said that no son of his was going to stay back a year and fall behind kids his own age. So Mike almost flunked first grade too, and second and third. He's been in and out of three schools already because Mom was always sure that if she and Dad could find the right system for him, he'd be a brilliant student. It was always the school's fault, never his.

"Lori, you're so short with me these days," Mom was saying. "It's as if we can't talk anymore."

"Good night, Mom."

As she closed the door, I wanted to call out to her to come back, to bring me a drink of water, to hold me like she did when I was little, before Mike took all her time.

"Tell me a story, Mommy," I used to say. And she would sit by my bed and tell me the story of how I was *chosen,* which means how they got me.

I used to love that story. I loved it because it was about me.

But I was too old for storytelling now. I had grown, but the story hadn't.

There was a faint scratching at the door, which could mean only one thing—Winkie had gotten trapped inside. I got up and opened it just wide enough to let him squeeze through. And then once again I made my way back to bed, put the pillow over my head, and tried to close out the world.

three

   It's hard to believe now, but all I knew about myself was in that chosen baby story.

   Once upon a time, the story went, there was a man and a woman (Mom and Dad) who wanted a child very much. But they couldn't have one. So they went to an agency in New York and asked the woman there if she would find one for them. And she said she would. While they waited, they bought a baby bed and pretty baby clothes, and painted a baby's room, and put fresh curtains on the windows. They were all prepared when the woman from the agency called to tell them to come right away—she had a baby for them. They raced to the agency so fast they almost got a ticket for speeding. The woman took them into a large room filled with rows of cribs, and they walked up and down until they saw me standing there in mine, holding my arms out to them. They knew right away that I was their little girl.

   I never wondered how a three-week-old infant was clever enough to stand up and hold out her arms, as if she wanted to be chosen by them. Or where all those babies came from. Still, even though it sounds corny, I preferred that story to all my picture books.

   I didn't catch on till much later that there was a lot missing from the story—like real facts. But when I asked my folks things like "Where are the baby's other parents now?" or, "Why did the baby's mother and father give her away?" they would act real strange. Dad would sort of clear his throat and find some reason to leave the room, and Mom's eyes would fill with tears. Then I'd feel guilty that I had made them feel so bad. I wouldn't ask any more for a while.

But I couldn't help thinking about it. Especially at night when I was in bed. I used to imagine that the baby (me) was a princess who had somehow gotten separated from her parents and was being raised by a good, loving couple (my adoptive parents).

The story had a few versions. In one, my real father was a wealthy prince who fell in love with a poor princess from another kingdom. His parents forbade him to marry her, but he did anyway. Secretly. When I was born they took me to the king, but instead of forgiving them, he banished me from the kingdom. He forced my father to divorce my mother and to marry a rich, ugly princess who had been picked out for him. Needless to say, my beautiful mother died of a broken heart, and my father killed himself, like Romeo did when he found Juliet lying in her coffin.

Sometimes when I was lying in bed at night I would weep when I got to the part where they died, and imagine that they were watching over me.

At other times, I was sure that both of them were still alive, still in love, and that they would eventually come to claim me. My real father was secretly sending money to my adoptive parents—that's how we could afford this big house. When the king died, and he took over the kingdom, my father would divorce his ugly, mean wife and marry my beautiful, gentle mother again. They would send for me, and we would all live together happily ever after.

Or something like that.

When I was about eight, the story took on more concrete form. I was home from school with a sore throat, sitting in the kitchen drinking cocoa while Mom was making chicken soup. Suddenly it popped into my head to ask her if she knew anything about my *other* mommy and daddy.

"They were fine people," Mom replied, continuing to cut the carrots as matter-of-factly as if we were discussing some close family friends. "You never have to worry about that."

"But why did they give me up? Why couldn't they keep me?"

"They loved you very much," she said slowly, looking down as if she was talking to the carrots. "They wanted to keep you, but they had no money. Your father was sick and out of work. So after you were born, they went to the agency and asked if there was a nice, childless couple who needed a little girl."

Mom was standing over the pot now, dropping the carrots into it. Her voice was coming out in short gasps, as if she were having trouble breathing.

"Go and see if there's anything on TV," she said at last. "The soup will be ready soon."

I thought a lot about my poor father and mother after that. Tears would well up in my eyes at the thought of them having to give up their baby. I saw my mother like a movie star in a Western, wearing old rags, her lovely face smudged with dirt. And my father looked like a film star too. He was always riding by on a large white horse. But when he got sick, he'd be lying on a narrow cot and she'd be sitting at his side.

MOTHER: *(Looking into an empty soup pot)* There's nothing to eat today. I'll have to go out and work or you'll never get well.

FATHER: *(With a tubercular cough)* But what about the baby? What will become of it? *(He gestures sadly toward the raggedy crib)*

MOTHER: I've already made plans. I've found a childless couple who will give it all the things we can't.

FATHER: Just in time. It looks so pale and thin now.

MOTHER: They need a baby. They'll make it plump and healthy, and buy it lots of toys. It will have a chance in life that we can't give it.

FATHER: I can die peacefully now.

I guess I went underground with my fantasies after that, until I was about twelve. I knew it was a subject we didn't talk about. But one night when I was sitting in the den alone with Mom and Dad, I heard myself saying, "Do you know what happened to my real parents?" The question seemed to come out of thin air, not out of me.

Dad looked up from his newspaper, and then he looked at Mom, who was knitting on the couch. He got up, put some Scotch in a glass on the bar, took a swig, and said hoarsely, "*We* are your real parents."

"The only ones you have to know about," my mother added in a strained whisper.

"You are *our* daughter," continued my father, speaking very formally in a voice I hadn't heard before. "You carry our name. You are an Elkins."

Then he choked, as if the Scotch had burned his throat.

I felt all choked up too. Mom must have felt sorry for me, because she put down her knitting and took off her glasses, the way she does when she's about to go into a long story.

"We don't know what became of your other parents," she said, "but I can tell you that your mother was a very pretty college girl."

"My God, Louise," my father interrupted sternly. He usually calls her Lou, so I knew he was really upset.

"It's all right, Harry, let me finish," she said firmly.

He left the room, but she went on.

"Your mother, as I said, was very bright and attractive, and . . . and she met someone she liked while she was a counselor at a summer camp. I think he was studying to be a doctor. They got married . . . but they hadn't planned to have a baby . . . they had to finish school . . . and they felt you'd be happier with a family who could really take care of you. The agency told us this when we came in to see you. You were so beautiful. We loved you at first sight."

Maybe she hoped that tacking the end of the chosen baby story onto the end of this new story would make it sound better. When I didn't say anything, she added, "But the important thing is that they were Jewish, like us. We're all part of the same family."

I went up to my room and threw myself down on the bed. Mom seemed to have forgotten the whole story about their being poor. Winkie was only a puppy then, and he raced upstairs after me, jumped on the bed, and started licking my face, as if he were trying to make everything all right.

I was getting confused again. I knew that Mom and Dad had met in a summer camp when they were in college. Was it possible they knew my parents? But I was born so much later. It didn't make sense.

I was afraid to ask any more questions. Mom and Dad didn't bring up the subject again.

And neither did I.

Until now.

four

When history rolled around again on Wednesday, I decided to play it cool. To stay loose. There wasn't much else I could do short of dropping out of school.

The tree was still on Mr. Innskeep's blackboard when we filed into the room, but some joker had drawn a skeleton hanging from it. Probably Bottomless Pit.

Mr. Innskeep just ignored it and all the snickers it caused. He walked back and forth, jiggling his chalk, and asked which of us "family explorers" (his words) wanted to start recounting what we had learned about our grandparents.

Some kids, like Whitney Smith, who is a grind no matter what she's grinding out, began waving their hands frantically. But Stephanie Jordan got his attention first.

"I tried to interview my grandmother last night, but she's totally bonkers," she said in her little baby voice. "She keeps her room totally locked all the time because she's afraid we'll come in and steal something. I knocked real politely and asked if I could talk to her about her childhood. She started shrieking that I couldn't have her jewelry and it took Mom totally the rest of the night to calm her down."

"That's a sad story, Stephanie. But it's a perfect example of what happens when we get to our sources too late," Mr. Innskeep commented. "Just think of the information that has disappeared forever because nobody tried to interview her before."

He sounded really sorrowful, as if Stephanie's grandmother

had just gone up in smoke, taking the national treasury with her.

Then Whitney told a long story about how her grandfather had come down from Alaska. He knew how to set bear traps back then, and even drove a dogsled. Now he's confined to his wheelchair and gets depressed when he can't take in the deer hunting season.

Usually when Whitney gives one of her long speeches her glasses keep sliding down her nose and I get so involved in watching her push them back up that I don't hear what she's saying. But I was listening now, to everything everyone said, as if I might hear something important to me.

Some of the stories about how their grandparents met were really funny. Bottomless Pit got down on his haunches and gave a wolf whistle when Sally Kingston told how hers got to know each other on a hayride out west.

"And how did *your* grandparents meet?" Mr. Innskeep asked Bottomless Pit, catching him off guard before he had a chance to get back to his chair. "Maybe you can top Sally's story."

For the first time, Bottomless Pit seemed at a loss for words. "I don't know," he said awkwardly.

It was obvious he hadn't given the assignment a thought.

"Come on now, your grandparents must have met." This got a few snickers, but it drove Bottomless Pit deeper into silence.

"Why, Jeffrey, I thought you were really into this subject, the way you were behaving," Mr. Innskeep said, half sitting on his desk, folding his arms in anticipation, the way he does when he's up to mischief.

This drew a blank too, but Mr. Innskeep didn't give up. He must have figured Bottomless Pit had it coming to him.

"Have you talked to your grandparents?"

"No."

"And why not, may I ask?"

"They're totally dead."

This got a big laugh, especially from Stephanie, who doesn't mind being teased, but it didn't distract Mr. Innskeep.

"Did you ask your parents about them?"

"They were out last night."

"And out the night before?"

"Yup."

"But you're going to talk to them tonight?" This came out more of an order than a question.

"I guess so."

"Good," said Mr. Innskeep, resuming his pacing. "We're looking forward to hearing what you learn."

I found myself feeling a little sorry for Bottomless Pit, because it was clearly hard for him to talk to his parents. I don't know anyone who really feels comfortable with their mother and father, like sitting down and really talking about things. Still he had it coming to him.

There were sad stories too. Edith Roth, who always speaks so softly you can hardly hear her, told how her grandparents had to flee Germany after Hitler came to power. A lot of her relatives were killed there, and she wouldn't have even been born if her grandfather hadn't insisted on leaving all their possessions and getting out.

It was just after Howie Gaines reported that his grandfather had been a bootlegger in Rhode Island that Mr. Innskeep took a long pointer and moved towards the blackboard.

"About this chap whom someone was kind enough to provide for me," he said, pointing to the skeleton as if he were about to give a lecture in anatomy. "You may find as you dig deeper that you have someone just like him on your family tree. Most families do. He's known as the skeleton in the closet. It may be hard for you to get your parents or other relatives to talk about him. But try. No matter how he behaved, no one can deny him a place on his family tree."

That really got to me. When you think of it, I had been removed from my original family tree. I was hanging on a tree I didn't belong on—biologically speaking. I wasn't attached in the way that other people are to theirs.

Hearing Mr. Innskeep go on like this made me feel even more of an outsider, as if I'd come from another planet. It reminded me of a fantasy I used to have while Mike and I were watching all those reruns of "Star Trek" on TV. Wasn't it possible, I thought, that both of us had come from somewhere in outer space? (Though we were so unalike that it must have been different galaxies.) I imagined myself like Superman on the planet Krypton just before it was about to explode. My parents were desperate to save me before it was too late.

FATHER: There are only a few minutes left until every-thing blows up.

MOTHER: I don't care about myself, but what about the baby—our baby—she should have a chance for life.

FATHER: There's a green planet down below. If we act immediately we can send her down in this small spacechute I've just designed.

MOTHER: Send her down alone? She would never survive!

FATHER: She has a chance. Which is more than she'll have if she stays here with us. The difference in the two gravities will break her fall.

MOTHER: But will someone find her and give her a home?

FATHER: Probably. Though they may not realize that she comes from another planet. But hurry, every minute counts now.

MOTHER: *(Putting baby tenderly into the spacechute)* My sweet baby, we must part now. But someday we will meet again.

FATHER: In another life.

MOTHER: But how will we recognize her?

FATHER: Her eyes.

MOTHER: Yes. We'll recognize her eyes.

FATHER: There she goes.

MOTHER: Farewell, my dearest baby. Until next time—

I was hurtling through space. The next voice I heard sounded peculiarly like Mr. Innskeep's.

"I said, Lori, if it's not too much trouble to come back to us from wherever you are, we would like to hear what you have learned from your grandparents."

He was standing right by my desk, staring at me. Everyone was staring. I could hear the flutter of peacock wings.

"I didn't get a chance to talk to anybody," I mumbled.

"Speak up, I can't hear you."

"My mother and father are out of town visiting my grand-father in the nursing home. He's very ill." I couldn't believe the lie, even as I said it.

"That's too bad." This with sympathy. "Well, speak to your parents when they feel up to it. Historians have to be persistent. They have to keep after their informants. If people don't want to talk, they have to guess why, and move in from another angle. They have to be ruthless, determined."

I began to understand why Mr. Innskeep enjoyed history. It meant being a snoop.

"History is not only in books," he was saying. " 'There is a history in all men's lives'—to quote from *Henry IV*. It is buried away in old trunks in attics and basements. It is hidden in closets and drawers. It is inscribed in old family Bibles and wills. In the course of this project we will learn how to go systematically through old ledgers at the town hall, how to track down missing relatives in cemetery listings and baptismal papers. We'll haunt reference rooms in the public libraries.

"And during spring vacation some of us may want to travel to Washington to go to the National Archives for naturalization records and ship passenger lists. . . ."

This last suggestion caused a stir of excitement in the room.

"We'll go not because the cherry blossoms are in bloom then, not in search of adventure, but in search of truth—not only about our families, but about ourselves," Mr. Innskeep concluded with a flourish.

After that, there was a lot of boring stuff—what kind of notebooks to buy for our interviews, how to keep special sections on the various members of the family, down to great-great-aunts and -uncles. We were also to keep a personal journal in which we jotted down facts about ourselves—like when we first walked and talked, and things we remembered enjoying or being frightened by.

"Your first memories are important," Mr. Innskeep said. "They hold hints about the way you behave now, the way you react to things."

As the bell rang, he called out, "There must be no secret that escapes my family explorers!" You would have thought he was an athletic coach sending his team onto the field.

Well, he wasn't going to have an easy time with me, I thought. I had managed to hold on to my secret a long time, and I wasn't about to give it up now, not in this class, with everyone ready to snicker or feel sorry for me—or even worse, to ask questions I wouldn't be able to answer.

By their very nature, roots are hidden in the ground. And I intended to keep mine hidden.

FIRST MEMORY

I am three and a half years old, all dressed up, waiting with Gram, who is staying with me, for Mom and Dad to come back from Boston. They are bringing a newborn baby who is also adopted. I am excited because Mom and Dad have talked about it for weeks, and I got my new dress for the occasion.

They come into the house carrying the baby. I expect it to be cute, like my doll. I'll be able to hold it and play with it. But it has an ugly little face, all red and screwed up. It's screaming its head off. I'm not even allowed to touch it.

Mom and Dad disappear into their bedroom with it and close the door. I want to follow them, but the door won't open. I hear the baby crying inside and I start crying outside as I pound on the door for my parents to let me in.

five

It's a funny thing about secrets. Sometimes when you do reveal them, no one will believe you. Like with Sue O'Brian, the girl next door who used to baby-sit for me and Mike. There's seven years' difference between us, and now that I'm sixteen and she's twenty-three, it doesn't seem to matter that much. But it did then.

I was a real chatterbox. I'd blabber on for hours, and once, to impress her, I blurted out that Mike and I were adopted. She told me to stop lying, and we had a big fight that ended up with my running to my room and refusing to come out.

But that didn't happen very often. She was really like my big sister and still is. I see her as much as I can, which isn't often since she has a full-time job with a veterinarian. It's the perfect job for her—she's an animal freak. Baby birds and squirrels always seem to choose the time she's passing by to fall out of their nests. And every stray cat for miles around must have her address, because hardly a week goes by without one appearing at her door.

That Wednesday when Maggie dropped me off, I noticed Sue's car in her garage and cut across the lawn to see her. I let myself in the front door, which was unlocked. Mrs. O'Brian always says in a fake brogue that a robber would have to be in his cups to break into their place. What she means is that their old house is so ramshackle compared to all the new ranch-style homes with picture windows and three-car garages that have sprung up like mushrooms in the fields all around it. The only reason their house is there at all is that it was there first, from the days when Mr. O'Brian's family were farmers. Now he works in the maintenance department at the local chemical plant. Mrs. O'Brian is a registered nurse.

Sue was in the kitchen cutting up some stew meat. She does all the cooking and cleaning for her dad while her mom is on a case. Her three older sisters are married, so the house is quiet compared to the way it used to be.

I stood in the doorway watching Sue for a few minutes, thinking how attractive she was. She used to wear her blonde hair long, in a ponytail, but now it's feathered around her face. Her pug nose is covered with freckles, which she hates, and there's a dimple in her chin which she also hates, but which I think is neat.

"Oh, you frightened me," she gasped when she looked up and saw me just standing there.

"I'm a ghost," I said.

"You look like one." She studied my face. "Anything wrong?"

I hadn't planned to tell her right away, but I heard myself spilling out everything about the history project and not knowing anything about my family tree.

She was quiet for a few moments. "You know, I thought you were making it up that time you told me you were adopted," she said quietly. "But Mom said she'd heard it from other people, and so it must be true."

"Your mom knew?" I said. "You never told me."

"Mom didn't think we should talk about it. Especially in front of your folks. The Elkinses are your family, after all. And they really love you."

"They're not my real family," I blurted out. And then the tears came again.

Sue took a Kleenex box off the windowsill and offered it to me like I was still seven years old.

"I really want to know where I came from," I sobbed, surprising even myself. It was the first time I had admitted to anyone that I was even curious.

"Does it really matter so much?" she asked gently, patting my head like I was some stray kitten that needed comforting.

"You're you, Lori Elkins, no matter who your real parents are."

I couldn't stop crying, because I knew it *did* matter, even though I couldn't explain why. All these years I had been able to act like it didn't. But now that I had started thinking about it —I mean really thinking about it—it was as if I had just awakened from a deep sleep.

"It matters to me," I wailed.

"Am I interrupting something?" a voice asked cautiously from the back door. It was Tony Daley, the law student Sue'd been going with the past two years. We hadn't heard his car pull into the driveway.

"I could come back later?" he said.

"Is it okay if Tony joins us?" Sue asked me.

I nodded yes, because I knew she would tell him everything anyway. He was over all the time. I thought they'd probably get married someday, though Sue never talked about it. I think it was because she still felt it would be unfair to Jim, the guy she was in love with in high school and was going to marry when he came back from Vietnam. Only he didn't come back. I thought she was going to die too, she was so sad. She wouldn't go out with anyone for a long time, until she met Tony at church. I knew she was going to be all right when she started fixing herself up again.

Tony's also a few years older than Sue but that's where his resemblance to Jim ends. Jim was blond and athletic, and Tony's very dark and studious. He'd been growing a bushy mustache to make himself look "dignified," because, he says, a lawyer has to impress his clients. It doesn't impress Sue too much (she says it tickles), but she doesn't object.

Now she filled Tony in on what we were talking about—my being adopted and not knowing what to do about my family tree. He was very surprised. He'd met my parents a few times, but this was the first time he'd heard about my being adopted.

"There was a kid on my block who was adopted," he said. "He never told us, but we all knew."

"How did you know?" I asked with a sniffle.

"I don't know, it's just something we knew. He was a strange guy, now that I think of it."

"In what way?" Sue asked.

"He always seemed distracted, as if he wasn't quite there," Tony replied, picking up Puffball, Sue's gray mother cat who was rubbing against his leg, and stroking her absently. "A loner. I used to wonder if it bothered him, not knowing who his real parents were. It would bother me."

"Would it?" I asked, kind of surprised.

"Sure it would. Wouldn't it bother you?" he asked Sue, handing her Puffball.

"I guess it would," she said slowly, giving Puffball a kiss between the eyes.

I couldn't imagine Sue not knowing her family. It was a huge clan. There were always O'Brians dropping by on Sundays, as if it was natural for them to gather together. Sue's uncle is a priest, and so sometimes the house is full of priests too. When I was much younger I would plead to go to Mass with Sue. I thought it was fun to get up early and kneel down seriously at the services. It was like a play and I was playing the part of an O'Brian. I even wanted an alabaster Madonna like theirs in our backyard.

Even though I didn't look like an O'Brian, it was easy to pretend I was one of them. Mom had said my parents were poor, and I could tell the O'Brians didn't have as much money as we did.

I imagined it like this. Mrs. O'Brian had me seven years after she had Sue. By that time, she and her husband had decided they couldn't afford another child. They were worrying about what to do with me when Mom and Dad just happened to come by looking for land to build on. . . .

MOM: (Seeing me in the baby carriage) How adorable she is!

MRS. O'BRIAN: If only there weren't too many mouths to feed here already. I don't know what to do.

MOM: We've been praying for a baby just like her for so long.

MRS. O'BRIAN: And I've been praying for a solution to my problem. I'm away on my nursing cases all the time now, and a baby needs a full-time

	mother.
MOM:	I'd be willing to be that mother.
MRS. O'BRIAN:	Then God has answered our prayers. She's yours.
DAD:	Can we give you something for her?
MRS. O'BRIAN:	Never. But I do have one condition: that you build on the land next door so we can watch her grow.
MOM:	We'll agree to that if you promise never to tell her that you are her real family. We want to be her only parents while she's growing up.
MRS. O'BRIAN:	It shall remain a secret.

I never did figure out how the agency got involved in that version. But my mind wasn't too logical in those days.

"You know, Sue, once I even thought I came from your family," I said now.

"I wish you had," she said, giving my hand a squeeze.

"I had to come from somewhere."

"Can't you ask your parents?" Tony said. "You're not a baby anymore."

"They don't like to talk about it."

"I can see how it would really hurt them," Sue told him. "They think of Lori and Mike as their own."

"Did they ever let anything about your real parents slip out —like their names?" Tony asked.

That really startled me. I had never thought about them having names like ordinary people. Or even faces. Just eyes. To me, they were fantasy figures, not real people out in the real world doing real things.

"Nothing," I said.

"That's hard then," he said sympathetically.

"There must be some way to learn their names," Sue said encouragingly, handing Puffball back to Tony. "Especially for someone with legal training."

"For instance?" said Tony.

"You."

"Wait a minute, this is getting heavy," he protested, dropping Puffball to the floor. She gave a squeal and ran off.

"Well, isn't it true that lawyers can find out anything they want to know?" Sue persisted playfully.

"Not quite," he replied, reaching for her hand and pulling her over to him. "There are some things that even lawyers can't do."

"But they must know how to search for missing people."

"Not so fast. Let's back up here," Tony said, glancing over at me. "Lori isn't going to rush out and search for her missing parents just because she has a history assignment."

My heart really took a lurch with that. Not only were they talking about the forbidden—my real parents—but now they were talking about searching for them. I sat there listening as if it all had nothing to do with me.

"Lori has to really think it through," Tony tried to explain.

"She's thought about it all her life, haven't you, Lori?" Sue said, getting carried away.

"I've wondered," I said lamely.

"Not the same thing," said Tony. "You have to really *want* to open up the past when you go searching. It's dangerous."

"How is it dangerous?" Sue asked.

"It's like opening a can of worms," he said. "You're taking a risk on what you'll find."

"Tony, I don't understand you," she exclaimed. "First you said *you'd* want to know, and now you're talking about worms and risks."

"You said yourself her parents would be hurt," he countered defensively.

They were going back and forth like that, as if I wasn't there.

"I just want us to help Lori in some way," Sue said at last.

"And I'm deliberately playing the devil's advocate," Tony admitted. "You learn in law to look at everything from all sides. Especially when it's something as delicate as this."

Then he turned to me. "Right, Lori?"

"I guess," I mumbled.

"What do you say? Would you like to know who your real parents are?"

"I think so."

"Think so. That's not enough."

"I mean I'd like to know about them. But I'm not sure I'd want to meet them."

Tony gave Sue an "I told you so" look.

"Is it because you'd feel guilty?" Sue asked me gently.

I nodded, the tears starting to well up in my eyes again.

"Poor baby, I can understand," she said, patting my head as if I had just fallen out of my nest. "You feel you don't have the right. Right?"

I nodded again, too choked up to speak.

"But you do have the *right*," Tony said now.

"I do?" I managed to ask. I'd never heard anyone say that before.

"You have a *moral* right. That's different from a legal one."

"Say that again," Sue broke in.

"What I mean is Lori has a human right to know how she got on this earth. But the law probably doesn't agree. If I'm not mistaken, birth records are sealed in almost every state in the union."

"Sealed?" I exclaimed. I pictured those sticks of colored sealing wax I used to drip on the envelopes of my letters.

"That's what it's called. It means that your records are locked away legally, and you can't see them without a court order. But I'm not sure if that's also true of the adoption orders."

"Adoption orders," I repeated. "What are those?" Boy, was I ever stupid in those days.

"Lori, you really are an innocent," Tony said, getting up and patting me on the head like Sue had done. "Adoption is a legal transaction, like marriage. Your adoptive parents couldn't get you without going to court and signing papers that made you legally theirs. Follow me?"

I nodded blankly.

"Those papers they signed have to be around somewhere —either in their possession or in the court's. I can look into all this if you want me to. Are you really serious about this?"

My head was nodding yes, but my heart was saying no. Fortunately, they could only see my head. Unfortunately, I didn't really know what I wanted. We all sat there in the kitchen listening to the stew bubbling in the pot, and watching Cleo, Puffball's daughter, walk across the counter sniffing hopefully.

"Some of the guys I know are in family law. I'll ask them," he said.

"For that you get a big reward—a taste of stew," Sue said, getting up to stir it.

"I want more than a taste," Tony replied playfully.

"No, you don't! You have to wait for dinner."

"We'll see about that," Tony cried, grabbing at her apron string. "See how she treats me?" he called, appealing to me.

Sue ran to the other side of the table, and he blocked her way with a chair. Cleo went scurrying out of the room.

I figured this was a good time for me to exit too. So I did.

Tony must have gotten to work right after I left, because he called me that night from Sue's.

"Lori, can you talk?"

"Sure."

"I mean, no one can hear?"

"I'm in my room."

"I asked around, and it seems that each state works differently. Some seal all the papers and some just the birth certificates. Do you know what state you were born in?"

"New York. Mom said they went to an agency there."

In my mind I heard her words: "We raced to the agency so fast we almost got a ticket for speeding." I'd always imagined them just driving down a Southhaven street, but now I realized they'd taken a long trip.

"I'll have to check into New York law then. If they're not sealed, do you have any idea where your parents would keep them?"

"No."

"It'd be too much to hope that they'd be around the house. They're probably in a safety-deposit box."

Sue took the phone here. "Hi, Lori."

"Hi."

"My grandmother used to keep all her treasures under her

mattress. You never know what crazy places people will think of."

She sounded like Mr. Innskeep then. That's the kind of thing he would say.

Tony took the phone again. "All right, Lori, you try the mattresses and I'll try the law books, and between the two of us we'll find either a leprechaun with a pot of gold, or your parents with a leprechaun."

Sue had the phone now. "Tony's a leprechaun in disguise!" A shriek came over the wire as if she were being tickled or tortured.

"Got to go now, 'bye!" she screamed with laughter, and hung up.

I knew that Maggie was out with her mother at an antinuke meeting, so I called Chris.

"If you had anything valuable, would you keep it under your mattress?" I asked, without even saying hello.

"Under *your* mattress," was his quick rejoinder.

"I'm serious."

"On *top* of your mattress."

"Chris, cut it out. Where would you keep it?"

"What are we talking about—jewelry?"

"We're talking about—uh, papers."

"Like deeds to houses and things?"

"Uh huh."

"In a safety-deposit box."

"Where else?"

"What is this, 'Twenty Questions'?"

"It's not a game—where else?"

"Lori, are you putting me on?"

"I need to know, Chris. That's all."

"Well, tell you what. Next Saturday night we'll have a long talk about it. Okay?"

"That's too late."

"We'll find a nice quiet spot where no one will disturb us."

"Good night, Chris. I'm hanging up." And I did.

The phone rang a few seconds later.

"Hello," I said.

"Hello, yourself. Are you mad at me?"

"No."

"Sure?"

"Sure."

"What's the question again? Where would I keep something valuable?"

"Forget I ever mentioned it, Chris."

"I never forget what you say, Lori."

"Well, forget this. I'm hanging up now."

"See you at school tomorrow?"

"Good night, Chris."

The next morning Maggie and I didn't have any classes together, so I slipped her a note in the hall:

I must ask you a question. A matter of life and death. Meet me at rear table in cafeteria at lunchtime.

Your anonymous friend

I got there before Maggie did.

"So tell me," she called, bounding over with her tray.

"Sit down," I said. "It will take time."

"I've got lots of time. What is it?"

Now that I'd gotten her so excited, I didn't know quite how to word it.

"Does your mother have a safety-deposit box?" I asked.

"Sure, for her jewelry," she said. "What does that have to do with anything?"

"Does she keep everything in it? Or does she hide some things around the house?"

"Lori, have you gone insane? Is that what you wanted to ask me?"

I must have looked sheepish, because she added, "I've been dying of curiosity all morning. I thought I'd never live till I got here. You said a matter of life and death."

"It is—for me."

She looked at me in exasperation.

"What do you mean?"

"I've got to find out where my parents keep their secret papers. My adoption records may be among them."

"So?"

"So, I want to see them."

Then she caught on. "I get it," she said. "You want to do some scouting on your own."

"That's right. Where would the logical place be to hide them if they were in the house?"

"Lisa keeps the things she doesn't want anyone to know about in her lingerie bags in the second right-hand drawer of her dresser."

"How do you know?"

"I've seen them."

"Maggie, you go through your mother's drawers?" I exclaimed.

"Lori, sometimes I don't believe you," Maggie muttered, pushing her tray away. "You mean you *don't* go through your mother's drawers?"

"No."

"Then start now. You never know what you'll find there. My first time, I didn't even know what I was looking for. But I've been doing it ever since I was tall enough to reach the handles."

"Ever find anything?"

"Not anything important. But I haven't given up hope."

"It . . . it seems so sneaky."

"Sure it's sneaky. But they're always hiding things from you. Controlling your life. You have to defend yourself. You have to know what cards they're holding so you can be prepared."

"Did you think you might find a picture of your father?" I asked, suddenly understanding what it was that Maggie was looking for.

She didn't answer, but started tearing strips from her paper napkin. "I figured she must have loved him once. She married him, didn't she? Had me. She must have kept some little thing to remember him by—a pressed corsage . . . a theater program. There must be something . . . somewhere."

She looked so wistful as she said it that I wanted to put my hand on her arm and tell her not to give up looking. But instead I heard myself saying, "Maggie, do you think I might find my adoption papers in some dresser drawer?"

"Anything is possible," she said. "Take a chance. Find out for yourself." And then her voice turned kind of hard. "You've got to be tough, Lori. You have to go after what you want. When they start dropping those bombs, it will be all over anyway, and you'll never find out the things you want to know."

Maggie always brought nuclear weapons into our conversations. She was always saying things like "We may not live a full life. We may have only a few years left. Once they drop those bombs . . ." It was because her mom was always organizing those antinuclear rallies and talking about the danger of a nuclear war. But now it dawned on me that I *did* want to know who I was before those bombs dropped. I didn't want to die not knowing where I came from.

"I'm going to look, Maggie," I said.

"What have you got to lose?" she asked, loading her dishes and the shredded napkin onto her tray. "The worst that can happen is that you won't find anything." And she added, "I'll keep my fingers crossed for you."

"Thanks, Maggie."

I was about to take off too when I spotted Chris wandering around with his tray, looking for me. "Over here," I called.

"My love is like a red, red, rose," sang Maggie. "See you in gym."

"Why are you hiding over here?" Chris asked, sliding his tray next to mine.

It was totally gross the way it was piled high with spaghetti and baked beans.

"Are you actually going to finish all that?" I asked.

"I am. And then I'm going to gobble you up for dessert."

"I'm not Little Red Riding Hood."

"Too bad. I'm the Big Bad Wolf."

"Aren't you ever serious, Chris?"

"What's to be serious about? Safety-deposit boxes?"

"Forget it."

"Life is too short to be serious. And I'm too tall."

He was always bantering like that. I could never really have a conversation with him. I figured it was just the California style, or because he was older, and cool. It was as if he wanted to keep me at a certain distance, even when it seemed like he was trying to be close. I was just as glad, because I wasn't about to confide in him either.

I can't remember whether it was Shakespeare or Mr. Innskeep who said something to the effect that timing has a lot to do with destiny. I thought I'd freak out at dinner that night when Mom said that she and Dad felt like catching a movie, and would I mind not going over to Sue's or anyplace else. She didn't call it baby-sitting anymore, but it was understood that I stayed in when they went out. My hand was shaking so much I could hardly hold my fork. I just kept my nose in my plate and answered any comments directed at me without looking up.

"Tell her not to bug me," Mike snarled as Mom and Dad were putting on their coats.

"Then go to bed on time," my father said sternly. "Ten o'clock. Not a second later."

We all knew it was a kind of game. Mike would go to bed when he felt like it.

Still, my father kept up pretenses, as if his saying "Go to bed at ten" would make it happen one night. As if he were still in control of things. My mother just nodded approval at his words, as if she too wanted to believe that they still carried some weight with Mike.

"Don't you stay up too late either, Lori," Mom said absently in my direction, almost as an afterthought.

"Good-bye," Dad called as he closed the door.

As soon as the car pulled out of the garage, Mike went into the den and turned on the TV. Immediately the sounds of shouting and gunfire filled the house, as if the set were plugged into all the destructive forces of the world.

I wondered what Mike would think if he knew what I was going to do. We never confided in each other; we certainly never talked about adoption. It was something we seemed to know we weren't supposed to do. As if it would be traitorous to Mom and Dad.

Would I have been able to talk to my *real* brother? Someone who was related to me by blood? Mike and I came from different parents, and we shared the ones we had now only by a fluke of fate—they had chosen us. I would never have chosen Mike for a brother, and I'm sure he would never have chosen me for a sister. We're very different. He's the mechanical type, stalking everything with walkie-talkies, assembling model trains and cars, making lights flash on and off with electronics kits.

He looked so lonely sitting there in the sickly gray light of the TV set. He couldn't really care about all those masked people running around with guns shooting at the police. For a moment I was tempted to give him a hint about what I was intending to do. But I restrained myself, because I knew he couldn't keep a secret. I'd learned to keep things to myself. It was better to let him remain in that murky world of cops and robbers that seemed to give him something he needed—if only an escape from himself.

I settled down on the couch in the living room and pretended to memorize my Spanish vocabulary. Winkie wandered about restlessly, not sure where to settle. At ten Mike flicked off the TV set and went upstairs without a word. At ten-thirty I heard him flush the toilet and then slam his bedroom door. Since Mom wasn't around to torture him with arguments about staying up, he was giving in to his fatigue.

I went to the foot of the stairs and called out as innocently as I could, "Night, Mike."

A muffled " 'Night," as if he were being strangled, came out in response.

I wasn't worried about him now. He always went right to sleep once he had gone to bed. We shared a great talent for sleeping. I knew I had just about half an hour—if that—before Mom and Dad came home. I tiptoed up the stairs, past Mike's room, and down the hall to their bedroom. My heart was pounding so loudly it sounded like a time bomb marking rhythm to my steps as I moved among the once-familiar objects that now seemed to have no relationship to me.

I rushed past my father's dresser as if he might jump out of it. Perched on top of it was a picture of Mike and me sitting with Winkie in the backyard. We looked like butter wouldn't melt in our mouths.

I was at Mom's dresser now. A bottle of her favorite perfume, Chanel No. 5, sat on top like a sentry.

I pulled out the top drawer carefully. There were the familiar gold and silver pins and bracelets, and the diamond necklace Dad got Mom for their last anniversary. A real thief would have grabbed that.

Second drawer: her underthings and the leotards she wears for exercise class.

Third drawer: sweaters. The were all in neat piles—unlike mine, which are always scrambled together in a heap. Her drawers are just like she is—orderly, precise, efficiently organized. Mom was an executive secretary for a big company before she got me. She'd never worked since, and she said she wasn't sorry she gave up her career. That raising children was big business in itself. An investment in the future. She disapproved of women who worked and left their children to be raised by other people. I guess she could have gotten the prize for Supermom of the Year—if there was one—because she was always waiting at home for us after school with milk and cookies, and driving us to all our activities. She acted as if we were the most important people in the world—other than Dad. And she still does. There are books all over the house on child development: the growing child from ages one to five, five to twelve, thirteen through sixteen. As if all the answers are in print. But I'd never seen any books about the adopted child. I guess she didn't think our problems were any different from those of ordinary kids.

I was on the bottom drawer now. Nightgowns—soft and feminine, but not too frilly. Like the rest of her clothes, they were more on the tailored and practical side. Again I ran my hands under everything and along the edges of the drawer. But this time I felt something—an envelope.

My heart almost stopped. Then it began beating so loudly I was sure Mike would hear and come racing in. Or that I'd faint dead away and my parents would come back and discover me lying there.

I sank to the floor and opened the envelope. It wasn't sealed.

There were two pieces of paper in it. The first was my birth certificate, which I had actually seen once before when I needed it for school. On it were my name, Loretta Elkins, the date and place of my birth, and then Mom's and Dad's names, as if I had been born to them. It never occurred to me to wonder why my real parents' names weren't on it.

The second paper, which I had not seen before, was marked ORDER OF ADOPTION in large letters. It stated that Baby Goldman (me), whose mother was Barbara Goldman, had been adopted by Louise and Harry Elkins through the Rocking Cradle agency in New York City. It was dated a year after my birth.

I didn't need to write anything down. It was branded on my brain. I would never forget the name: Barbara Goldman.

I put the papers back in the envelope and the envelope back under the nightgowns, being careful to make everything look as neat as before. Then I rushed to my room feeling like a thief, Winkie fast on my heels.

I had stolen my real mother's name.

I dived into bed and lay there holding Winkie in my arms. He's not allowed on the bed, let alone *in* it, so he must have been very surprised. "Barbara Goldman," I whispered into his long golden ear, and got a wet lick on my cheek in return. Seeing my mother's name, and mine listed as Baby made me realize I'd really been born. I had not just magically appeared on this earth, but had come from a real flesh-and-blood mother. Whose name was Barbara Goldman.

Not too long afterwards I heard our car pull into the driveway. Winkie squirmed out of my arms and began scratching impatiently at my door. The traitor. I let him out and then crawled back into bed. I heard the garage door shut and the tread of my parents' footstep on the stairs.

"Down boy!" came Dad's usual response to Winkie's flying leaps of welcome.

I hoped they wouldn't notice anything different in their room. I closed my eyes so that if Mom peeked in she would think I was asleep.

Hot tears burned my eyes; I buried my face in my pillow to stifle the unexpected sobs that were coming from my throat. I didn't know who I was crying for. Was it for Baby Goldman? Or for that lost mother I'd never known—Barbara Goldman?

Or was it for Lori Elkins, who, I knew, would never be the same again?

six

Maggie was late to school the next day, so I slipped her a note in music.

Maggie mia,

Mission accomplished. Dug some roots. Wire congrats to Baby Goldman c/o the Rocking Cradle.

Soon I got back:

Rocking Baby mia,

Congrats on new birth, new parents, new identity. Get yourself a security blanket and keep crawling.

Adios, Mama Maggie

To which I replied:

Maggie mia,

I need a pacifier. I'm afraid of the dark.

Rocking Baby

And she answered:

Baby mia,

Fear not. Trust Mama mia. Your family tree is over the next hill.

And I replied:

When the bough breaks, the cradle will fall,
And down will come baby, cradle and all.

I should have been happy, but I wasn't. My head was splitting.
And I kept having hot and cold flashes—as if something
terrible was going to happen.

"Something totally *wonderful* is going to happen," Maggie
assured me on the way home from school. "You've just got a
case of the jitters. It's not every day you find your mother's
name. Now all you've got to do is find the woman who goes
with it."

She said it as if it was the most natural thing in the world
—going out and finding my mother. How could I explain to
her that I wasn't sure I wanted to find her—or my father? I just
wanted to know who they were. That was all.

I couldn't even explain it to Sue and Tony that night.

"Barbara Goldman . . . Barbara Goldman." Sue was test-
ing the name on her lips, like I had been doing ever since I'd
seen it. "She sounds like a nice person. I like her already."

Tony said, "I like Baby Goldman, too."

And we all laughed. It seemed funny for that moment, not
heavy like before.

"And what's your father's name?" Sue asked.

My father's name. I hadn't even realized it was missing until
then.

"I didn't see it," I said.

"It had to be there," Tony said.

"It wasn't," I insisted.

Tony stopped arguing the point.

"Maybe he was away in the army, or died before Lori was
born," Sue said.

"We'll track him down somehow," Tony said.

My head started throbbing again. I might have wondered
about those lost parents, but I had never thought I could meet
them as if they were real people like everyone else. And—this

really scared me—how could I be their daughter and the daughter of my folks at the same time? I had to be one or the other. Or be split down the middle.

I suddenly wanted to cling to Lori Elkins. She was all I had.

seven

"I hope you're keeping detailed notes on all your research," Mr. Innskeep kept reminding us. "I'm going to look through them one of these days—so be warned. Remember to keep searching for new information all the time. Never relax. Tomorrow, tomorrow, and tomorrow you may find the vital piece of information you need for your family tree."

It was only the beginning of February, but already there was a sign-up sheet on the bulletin board for those who wanted to go on the spring vacation research trip to Washington. Hortense's name was the first one down. She was planning to visit the Daughters of the American Revolution—otherwise known as the DAR—for more facts about her Pilgrim ancestors. A few of the other kids were going to check out the National Archives to find out what boats their ancestors had come over on. Whitney was going to the Bureau of Indian Affairs because she'd learned that her great-grandmother might have had some Cherokee blood.

There was also a sheet for those planning to go in to New York. Edith was going to a library called YIVO, which has archives on the Jewish communities that perished in the Holocaust. Stephanie Jordan was totally excited about going to the big public library to visit its genealogical department.

"I ought to put up a sheet for adopted kids who want to go in search of their lost parents," I told Maggie that afternoon at her house. "That would really blow Mr. Innskeep's mind."

"That's not a bad idea," said Maggie. "I'll do the itinerary for it. In fact, I know where the first stop should be."

"Where?"

"The Rocking Cradle agency."

That took me by surprise. "Why there?"

"For information about Barbara Goldman, dum-dum. They probably have as many files in that place as the FBI."

We were sitting in her room while she experimented with her hair in front of the vanity. It has a three-way mirror, and if you adjust it in certain ways you can see all sides of your head at the same time. Maggie could stay there for hours parting her hair in the middle, pulling it up on one side, or piling it on the top of her head. Now she was braiding two long strands with brightly colored beads.

"If I were you I would definitely get me to that agency," Maggie was saying.

"Maggie, I wouldn't dare."

"Don't be an idiot," she said, concentrating more on a blue bead than on me. "What can they do to you? Put you back in the cradle again?"

"I mean, I just wouldn't have the nerve to walk in there."

"You could write for an appointment first."

"What if they tell my parents?"

"Lori, they probably haven't been in touch with your parents for sixteen years."

"I wouldn't know what to say in a letter."

Maggie was never at a loss for words. Or courage. "I'll write it for you," she said, giving the braids a final approving pat. "Like it?"

She looked like one of those African queens in the movies.

"Well, it's . . . original."

"Lisa will probably say it's overdone for my age and make me undo it."

"Won't it hurt to sleep on?"

"I'll arrange my head very carefully on the pillow and then will myself not to move all night. The way I will myself not to have a midnight snack." Then she turned to look at me. "Do you want me to write the letter for you? I can do it in Esperanto, Latin, Spanish, or Old English full of thee's and thou's."

"Maggie, be serious. It's not funny."

"Well, do you?"

"Yes."

I was being such a coward, which was weird, because I'm very brave about most things, like trying out for plays and interviewing people for our school newspaper. Once I even went to see our state senator about his new education bill. And now I had just gotten the lead part (Emily Webb) in the school's spring production of *Our Town* by Thornton Wilder. Maggie got the part of Mrs. Webb, my mother, and here I was leaning on her as if I really was her child.

"Don't worry, Baby, I'll write a terrific letter."

She was calling me Baby a lot now. It started as a joke, but somehow it didn't seem so funny anymore.

"Why do you think they didn't give me a name?" I asked, trying on the Indian wrap skirt I saw on Maggie's chair.

"Maybe they couldn't think of one," she said. Then, seriously: "Maybe the agency forgot it. Or wanted your adoptive parents to give you one of their own. I like Lori."

"It's short for Loretta, which I hate. Do I have this skirt tied right?"

"Yes, but be careful of it. It's Lisa's. She doesn't know I've borrowed it yet. Do you know the address of the agency?"

"No . . ."

She picked up the phone, dialed New York information, and asked for the number of the Rocking Cradle. Then she dialed the number and in a very affected high-society type voice, she asked the switchboard operator for the name of the director, and the address. I couldn't believe it. She made it sound so simple. It was like dialing directly into the past.

"I'll do the letter tonight," she said.

"Maggie, you're fantastic."

"It's nothing. Now, should I put another bead on this braid, or not?" she asked, turning once again to the mirror.

Maggie handed me the letter in the hall before school the next day. She'd typed it on her new Smith-Corona electric portable. It was very short, but she said it took her hours because she kept hitting the wrong keys:

Dear Ms. Barnes:

   I was adopted from your agency sixteen years ago. I am very happy in my adopted family, but I would like to know something about my real parents. Could I please make an appointment to come in and see you?

Sincerely yours,

"All you have to do is sign it and stick it in the mail," she said.

I pulled out a pen and balanced the letter on my notebook. I wrote my name as carefully as I could so Ms. Barnes wouldn't think I was immature or falling apart. I felt like I was signing my death warrant. Handing the letter back to Maggie as if it were a hot potato, I said, "You mail it. I can't."

"Boy, are you ever helpless," she said. But she took the letter and stuck it into her bookbag. "I'll put the return address care of me. Otherwise, your folks might see—"

"See what?" Chris asked, coming up from behind.

"Wouldn't you like to know?" Maggie teased.

"There are lots of things I'd like to know," he replied. "Like why you and Lori have so many secrets."

"What secrets?" I asked, trying to sound innocent.

"That's what I'd like to know."

"We've been talking about our parts for the play," Maggie said. "You are speaking to Mrs. Webb, who is, among other things, Lori's mother."

"You mean you're my new mother-in-law?" exclaimed Chris, falling against the wall in mock dismay.

"Yup. And you'd better watch yourself, young man."

eight

Maggie was a natural for the part of Mrs. Webb. She really digs character roles.

"Emily, come and help me string these beans for the winter," she'd say in a high falsetto voice before rehearsal started. (She liked that line a lot.) "George Gibbs let himself have a real conversation, didn't he? Why, he's growing up. How old would George be?"

"I be ninety going on a hundred," Jack Wyler, who was playing George, would chime in. And we'd all go into hysterics, as if he'd said the funniest thing in the world.

Jack's father is the most expensive dentist in town, and he's written two best-selling books: *Learning from Your Wisdom Teeth* and *The Gravity of Your Cavity*. He makes you feel that your teeth will rot and fall out if you don't concentrate on them full-time. I knew Maggie was really hooked on Jack when she started buying dental floss. By the end of that first week of rehearsals they were nibbling on each other's ears. I'd have to call out, "Hey, George, remember, you're going to marry *me*."

Jack was shorter than Maggie—he had a stocky body that was built low to the ground like a bulldog—but he made up in wit for what he didn't have in height.

"Emily, it's your loss if you don't floss!" he'd say, crossing his eyes, when we'd begin a scene together. Or "Don't pout if your teeth fall out."

I liked being Emily. It was another identity to add to my own. She was unusually close to her mother. She seemed to enjoy stringing beans with her in a way that I never could with mine. In that scene she asks, "Mama, am I good looking?" And her mother answers, "Yes, of course you are. All my children have got good features. I'd be ashamed if they hadn't."

It always freaked me out when Maggie said that line. Emily's family was just an ordinary one in a small New Hampshire town at the turn of the century, but her mother took their looking alike for granted—because they belonged to each other by blood. I really love my mom, but I can't speak as freely to her as Emily does. I guess because there are all those unspoken things between us.

But, to be honest, I was so deep into myself those days, I was finding it harder and harder to speak freely to anyone, except Maggie. I had to force myself to act carefree— especially with Chris.

Jack and Chris were kind of friends, since they were both seniors on the swimming team. The four of us started hanging out together in the cafeteria and at the Fiery Ox on weekends when the team was in town. They were all so busy clowning around, I was sure that Chris wouldn't notice how out of it I was feeling.

But he did.

We were sitting in the library during my free period before history, doing our homework. Or, rather, he was doing *my* math. I could never get involved in problems like, If A went so many miles and met B, and they both traveled so many hours and had so much gas—after X number of miles, how much had they paid? My head didn't work that way.

"A penny for your thoughts," Chris said, running his hand slowly down my neck and across my back. I liked the feel of his hands. They always seemed to know what they were doing —even though they weren't doing very much.

Chris and I may not have been sleeping together, but some kids in our class were. Molly Pendleton got pregnant and had to leave school last November. Maggie said she was really stupid to have gotten knocked up. I said it was just bad luck. I knew one of the reasons I hadn't gone all the way with anyone was not that I was so virtuous, but that it would be just my luck to get pregnant too.

"In this day and age it's dumb," Maggie insisted. "All she had to do was go to the doctor, with or without her mother, and get the Pill. Or something."

Maggie had an IUD. You know, one of those things that gets placed inside you for good. Lisa said she'd rather have Maggie prepared than pregnant. She also said she'd rather Maggie use her room at home than stay out in parked cars.

But my mother never talked about these things with me. I think it embarrassed her. Sometimes when I got in late, I'd see the light on in her room and know that she was worried. It was almost as if she had the fear that I was doing something bad out there.

It's strange about parents. Maggie could talk to Lisa about almost anything, but she couldn't talk to her about her father. It was her mother's secret place that couldn't be touched.

"I said, 'Penny for your thoughts,'" Chris repeated, this time chewing on my finger.

"They're worth more than a penny," I retorted, wondering if he had secret places too. He'd never told me anything about his parents, except that they were on that trip around the world. But then, boys don't talk much about their feelings. They seem to prefer throwing balls at each other.

"Your math grade isn't going to be worth a penny if you don't start concentrating on this problem," Chris said. I think he enjoyed playing teacher. He was really a lot smarter than he let on. It was almost as if he had to act like he didn't care about all those schools he had been kicked out of and the incompletes he was making up now.

"I hate money," I said, stretching in the chair. I did, too. I planned to live in a garret in New York someday, no matter how successful a writer or actress I became.

"That's because you have it," Chris said, taking me seriously. "If you had to be on your own, you'd feel differently."

"Have you ever been on your own?" I asked, realizing that this was turning into a serious conversation—the first one I'd ever had with him.

"I tried to be," he said. "But my old man kept forcing me

back to school. If I had my choice I'd be working in California now. But he wants me out of there. Said it ruined my brother."

"Did it?"

I was surprised. He'd never mentioned a brother before. But he obviously wasn't going to elaborate. He stood up and started packing up his books.

"Let's get some air before the next class," he said. "I've got a physics test coming up."

We met Maggie in the hall.

"Hi, Chris. . . . 'Bye, Chris," she added, as the bell rang.

"See you 'round," he said, walking off.

"What's the matter with him?" Maggie asked.

"His brother, I think."

"His brother? I didn't know he had one."

"Neither did I."

However, Maggie had more important things than brothers to worry about. We had moved from reporting on grandparents to parents in history, and though she was lucky enough not to have been called on yet, she was sure her luck was running out. Mr. Innskeep had announced a new plan to go through the class alphabetically, beginning with the boys, and alternating with each letter. It wouldn't take long to get to Brooks.

She was still undecided about whether it was honest to hang Alan on her father's spot as if he belonged there.

"I'm tempted to leave the paternal side of my tree blank," she said. "As if I'd just sprung full blown out of some Greek goddess's head—"

"Whose name was Lisa."

"Right. Or I could put Zeus down as my father and blame everything on him. He was always seducing human maidens."

"Like Lisa?"

"No, I guess not. Lisa would never fall for Zeus no matter what his disguise. He was too warlike. She likes them contemplative—like Alan."

"And your father," I reminded her.

"Yeah, and my father. Whatever he was like."

"You still can't ask her about him?"

"Impossible," she said.

We both knew that Lisa had a tendency to drink too much if

she got upset. She could take the world's problems on her shoulders, but anything personal really threw her. Once when we went to Maggie's place after school, Lisa had had a fight with Alan, and was staggering all over the living room, making funny remarks that weren't really funny. Maggie was mortified, but she was worried too, because she knew that when her mother went on a binge like that, it could last for days.

"Lisa's always on a delicate balance," she added.

"Yeah, I understand," I said.

Her not knowing was like my not knowing, though at least she had one real parent. "But you have the *right* to know, if you want to," I added, thinking of Tony's words to me. "He was your father."

"Maybe she'll tell me someday when she's ready," Maggie said. "I've made myself not ask about it all these years. I've never told you, but his parents live around here."

"You mean your grandparents?"

She nodded.

"How do you know?"

"It just slipped out once a few years ago when Lisa and I were arguing about something. I can't even remember what."

"And they never came to see you?" I was amazed.

"Lisa said they don't want to see me."

"Do you know their address?"

"It's really close—in Andersonville. I check the phone book when the mood hits me to see if they're still listed. It's a way of knowing if they're still alive."

Maggie's voice had dropped to a whisper, because kids were pushing past us into Mr. Innskeep's class and she didn't want anyone to hear. "I'll die if he calls on me," she moaned. I put my hand on her shoulder as we went into the room. "Maybe he won't get to you today," I said.

As it turned out, he didn't. Mr. Innskeep had decided against the alphabetical idea and said he just wanted to hear from some of the boys. The first one he called on was Bottomless Pit. I was sure he'd just clown around like last time when he said his grandparents were "totally dead." Mr. Innskeep had let him off the hook after that, and I was just waiting to hear what kind of wisecracks he was going to make about his parents.

But Bottomless Pit didn't seem up to fun and games this time. He didn't even seem like himself. He was, if anything, more awkward than usual, tripping over the leg of his chair as he started down the aisle. Almost falling. Ordinarily he would have made a big joke out of that—or at least given a gesture of mock terror. But now he just proceeded silently to the front of the room.

Once there, he looked down so we couldn't see his face. Then he looked up at the ceiling, as if we were all sitting up there. And he said haltingly, "I don't know how my parents met, or anything about them. I don't even know who they are. I'm adopted."

I wasn't the only one stunned. There was complete silence in the room, as if Bottomless Pit had announced that he was going to stop eating or something.

Even Mr. Innskeep seemed at a loss for words. Then he tried to put Bottomless Pit at ease with a lighthearted comment: "Well, I hope you have a green thumb. You're going to have to graft another tree right onto your main trunk."

It went over like a lead balloon. Bottomless Pit just stood there turning redder and redder as if he were on fire, and no one said anything. My face was burning too. I buried it in my hands so it wouldn't give me away.

"There's nothing to graft," Bottomless Pit said at last.

Mr. Innskeep tried a new approach. "I've never known anyone who was adopted, Jeffrey, but I'm sure there must be something. Everyone was born to someone. Just ask your adoptive parents."

"They don't like to talk about it," Bottomless Pit managed to say in a cracked voice.

"Then you have asked them already?"

"Years ago. They said they didn't know anything."

"Well, now that you're older they'll probably be happy to give you all the information you want," Mr. Innskeep tried to reassure him. "Especially when they learn it's for your history assignment."

Bottomless Pit just swallowed hard. He didn't look very convinced.

"Surely they've told you something," Mr. Innskeep continued, like someone trying to start up a fire in a cold stove.

"Just that when they got me I was very sick. I would have died if they hadn't taken care of me."

"And how did they get you?"

"I don't know."

Poor Bottomless Pit. I really felt sorry for him. Mr. Innskeep might know a lot about Shakespeare, but he didn't know anything about adoptive parents.

"They've never told you where you were born?"

"No. Just that the hospital burned down a long time ago."

"I don't think it's common for a hospital to burn down," Mr. Innskeep said, the historian in him trying to come to terms with this new fact.

"Well, this one did," said Bottomless Pit.

He sounded so pathetic, I had to look up. I realized how nice-looking he was when he was serious like this. His eyes were really a pretty blue, and if he took off one of his chins, he wouldn't be half bad.

No one said anything for a while, and Bottomless Pit just stood there shifting his weight from one leg to the other. For a moment, he even looked as if he might burst out crying. Maybe he would have if Mr. Innskeep hadn't said with a burst of inspiration, "Well, Jeffrey, forget I ever mentioned the grafting. Just fill in your adoptive family's tree."

That really broke the tension in the room.

"Yeah, I'll do that," Bottomless Pit responded, as if Mr. Innskeep had suggested some fabulously original idea. He looked so relieved you'd think his head had just come off the chopping block.

Then Stephanie spoke up in her little baby voice, even though she hadn't been called on. "I *totally* agree. They are your *real* parents."

"That's right. They sat up with you all night when you were sick," Sally called out.

And then they were all talking at once, reassuring Bottomless Pit that it didn't matter who his other parents were.

"They didn't care about you, so why should you care about them," said Judith.

"You should be grateful your parents adopted you, or you would have been an orphan," said Whitney.

I didn't say anything, of course. Didn't even dare look over at Maggie for fear someone would notice how flushed I was. What really got me was that no one suggested that Bottomless Pit might be curious about who his real parents were. People who know their real parents never think about things like that. Even Mr. Innskeep, who thinks about so many things, didn't think of it.

Then I had a horrible thought. If Mr. Innskeep was jumping around now, he could easily jump over to me next time. And I didn't have the remotest idea what I was going to say. I just knew I wasn't going to confess the way Bottomless Pit had. But what *was* I going to do?

Until now I had been hoping I'd know when the moment came, while praying that moment would never come. It was like magical thinking—if I pretend it's not going to happen, it won't.

But I couldn't pretend anymore. I had to think of something —fast.

nine

Mom met me at the door as I came home from rehearsal later that week.

"Lori, do you think you could talk to Mike?"

"About what this time?"

All I needed now was Mike. I haven't mentioned that besides everything else, Mike is a kleptomaniac. Last fall he was caught shoplifting in one of the small stationery stores near his school, and the month after that he was suspended for a few weeks for setting fire to the wastepaper basket in the gym. I guess that makes him a pyromaniac too. He was seeing a shrink twice a week now instead of once. Mom had been crying a lot when I wasn't around. I could tell by the red rims around her eyes. She must have been wondering where she had failed. Mike seemed so angry and frustrated all the time. But then he had been pretty destructive when he was little too—I remember how he used to tear the limbs off my dolls, and scribble all over my favorite books. He was always breaking things, even things he made himself and cared about.

Mom was saying, "Oh, Lori, if you'd just talk to him. He came home and slammed his door and locked it, and he won't let me in. Something terrible must have happened. You used to be able to get him out of bad moods. Please try."

I had almost forgotten. There'd been times when Mike and I were close. I'd try to help him with those electrical kits he was always assembling, even though I was all thumbs. He really had magic fingers when he made things. "We need people like you," I'd tell him, trying to bolster his ego. "If the world were

60

made up of people like me we'd be sitting in the dark all the time, because we wouldn't know how to harness electricity to make light, or how to send spaceships to the moon."

I'd ramble on like that—and really mean it—but it's no use explaining to people like him how much they're needed, when they get the message in school that they're dumb.

"Okay, I'll try talking to him if he'll let me in," I said. "But I have to put my things down first."

I went to my room and slowly took everything out of my bookbag. Then I washed up in the bathroom and my eyes said hello to the eyes in the mirror. "Did you have a good rehearsal, Lori?" my eyes asked.

"The name is Emily Webb," I told my eyes.

I brushed my hair thoroughly, more times than I had to, because I really dreaded having to go into Mike's room and act the big sister. We were almost like strangers these days. I'd been so busy with school, and he'd been so busy getting into trouble.

Finally I knocked on the door.

"Are you there, Flug? It's me, Fro."

We once made up a whole family of trolls who lived in his closet. He was Flug, and I was Fro. I suppose it really was like a game of house in the beginning, the older troll taking care of the younger one, but we seemed to take naturally to making ourselves into unreal creatures. Then the game somehow merged with one that was going around called "D & D" —"Dungeons and Dragons." Usually Flug would play the dungeon master, leading me through a labyrinth of doors behind which there would be various monsters. My powers had to match the powers of these evil creatures.

There was no response from Mike, so I knocked again. "I'm using the knock spell," I said.

"I'm casting the wizard lock," he replied.

"Then I'm casting my most powerful spell if you don't open up," I said.

Miraculously, the door opened. Mike was already back on his bed, face to the wall, when I stepped inside.

"How many dragons and wicked wizards did you overpower today?" I asked.

"Three warlocks and one witch."

"Mom's crying as if you got her too."

"That's her business. She's not in the game."

"You can't keep her out of it, Flug. She's got her special powers too."

He put his head in his arms, as if he was already defeated.

"I'm using the super-powerful word that forces you to do what I say."

"Which is?"

"Talk."

"There's nothing to talk about."

"Tell me or die."

"You'd only go blabbing to Mom and Dad."

"I won't. If you don't want me to. Cross my heart with dragon blood."

He sat up and looked at me glassily, as if he were trapped in his dungeon. "I don't care what you do. They'll find out soon enough. I got suspended from school today."

"Again?"

Our eyes met for a moment like they used to when we were conspiring about some maneuver in the game, and the humor of it struck us both at the same time. We began laughing hysterically. I mean really laughing, from way inside. Mike let out loud whoops, like howls of joy (which of course were really pain), and I sank to the floor gasping and choking as I tried to stop. One thing Mike always had was a sense of humor, and there were just so many times we could play his getting suspended from school as high tragedy. Tragedy and comedy are two sides of the same coin, as Miss Lathem, our drama coach, is always telling us.

"What for this time, mighty Flug?" I managed to get out.

"Someone found pot in my desk."

Again we went into shrieks of laughter.

"And . . . and took it to the Wizard."

"And?"

"And he took it to the Super Wizard."

We couldn't talk anymore, we were so doubled up.

"And it wasn't even mine."

I stopped laughing. "It wasn't?"

"No. Someone has it in for me."

"Flug, are you telling me the truth?" I wanted to believe him. All these years I had wanted to believe him, but he had disappointed me so many times.

"Don't believe me, I don't care."

"I believe you, Flug. Tell the Super Wizard it wasn't yours."

"I did. He said I was responsible for its being there."

"Tell the folks."

"It doesn't matter anymore. What difference does it make who put it there? No one will ever believe me."

There was a knock on the door. Mom put her head in. Her face had a hopeful, expectant look. "Did I hear laughter coming from in here?"

"Wrong again," said Mike. "Will the two of you please get out? Now."

This last was a sharp command. The spell was broken. And so was my power. Mike turned his face to the wall again.

I left behind Mom. Equally defeated.

"Good-bye, mighty Flug," I called back to him. And it really did seem that I was parting from someone who was moving deeper and deeper into the dark recesses of a dungeon.

I told Mom what Mike had told me because I really believed him and wanted her to also. Then I went to my room. I could hear her phoning Dad at the office and telling him what had happened.

Sue came over later that night.

"Tony's so busy right now I hardly see him," she said. "But he told me to tell you he hasn't forgotten your project. He's going to talk to some of his professors about adoption legislation. He'll be a real expert by the time he's finished."

She was sitting on my bed, leafing through my playscript with one hand, petting Winkie with the other. "Beautiful," she kept murmuring. I didn't know which she meant.

"I'm going to come and see you in it."

She meant the play.

"Even if it's on a night I'm scheduled to work."

"Bring the animals with you."

"We have a mynah bird in the clinic now. He can do a wolf whistle just like a real person."

"Then definitely bring him."

"He has a cold, poor thing. He was lying on the bottom of his cage when his owner brought him in. I was sure he was finished. But Dr. Gallagher pumped antibiotics into him and we've been putting liquid vitamins down his gullet four times a day. This morning he was up on his perch again, whistling louder than ever."

"Tell him to keep practicing for opening night. Then the critics will say our play is for the birds."

"The critics will be wolf-whistling too, I know it."

"Thanks, Sue. For everything."

"Don't thank me. Tony's the one digging into things."

"He's really great, Sue."

"I know." But her eyes got kind of distant, as if she'd thought of Jim even as she said it. "We've got to go after the things in life that can still be recovered," she said. "Before it's too late."

And then she added, "Remember how Jim used to carry you around on his shoulders as if he was a horse? You were so scared at first. But after that you wanted a ride every time you saw him. 'Trot,' you'd command. 'Gallop!' You were so bossy. You'd just wear him out."

She was smiling now, as if it was happening right there in my room.

I had never talked to Sue about Jim after he was brought back wrapped in a flag, like a hero. I thought it would hurt Sue if I even mentioned his name. But now I realized that she had been wanting to talk about him all along. And I understood why she wanted Tony to help me find my lost parents. Before it was too late.

ten

I was sure an answer from the Rocking Cradle agency would never come. Dad's phrase, "Don't count on it," kept going through my mind. I'd never really thought about what not counting on something meant. I usually got the things I wanted, and just took it for granted that I always would. But now that my old familiar world was slipping away from me —or was I slipping away from it?—I was beginning to understand how profound those words were.

Our house had now changed from gloom to doom. Even though the principal had decided to believe Mike about the pot and he was back in school again, he wasn't acting much better. Sometimes he'd just play hookey and Mom wouldn't know it until the school called to find out if he was sick. He stayed in his room a lot when he was home, poring over his "D & D" monster manuals and making elaborate dungeon maps instead of doing his homework. I stayed away from the house as much as possible.

When I wasn't at rehearsal after school, or with Chris, I went over to Maggie's. But I couldn't seem to talk about anything except when the letter from the agency was going to come.

"We can't just sit around waiting," Maggie exclaimed one day. "Let's do something!"

"Like what?"

"Like try to find Barbara Goldman on our own."

"Maggie, be serious."

"I've never been more serious in my life. We're family

explorers, aren't we? Mr. Innskeep said start with the obvious things first. So let's explore the New York phone system."

"Why New York?"

"Because that's where she gave you up. She might still be there—grieving."

"But even if she were, the listing would be under her husband's first name, not hers. And we don't know it."

"What if she was a feminist?" Maggie argued. "Then she would have kept her maiden name, Goldman, when she married. And we'll find it listed under Barbara."

It was really wishful thinking, but I liked that image of my mother. A strong, independent woman.

"But we don't have a New York phone book," I said, still the defeatist.

"Ever hear of Information, idiot? We make the operator do the work for us."

She picked up the phone and dialed Manhattan Information as casually as if she were calling a friend. "Operator, do you have any Barbara Goldmans listed? Yes, G, as in God. No, I don't have an address."

There were six Barbaras and ten B's.

Then she got the listings for three other New York boroughs —Brooklyn (nine Barbaras and twelve B's), the Bronx (two Barbaras and three B's), and Queens (one Barbara and two B's).

"Let's try Manhattan first," Maggie said.

"Brooklyn has the most Barbaras," I pointed out.

"'But only the dead know Brooklyn,'" she responded, quoting her favorite author, Thomas Wolfe.

Maggie didn't understand that for me, my mother dwelled more in the world of the dead than the world of everyday life. I wasn't eager to go on with this.

"It's going to be expensive to call from here," I said. "It's long distance."

"If Lisa complains about the bill, I'll say it was a survey I had to do for Jack's father. 'Madam, do you floss your teeth every time you say a dirty word?'"

Maggie had a way of making everything into a game—even something as earthshaking as searching for Barbara Goldman.

She pulled the phone onto the bed and sat cross-legged on it while dialing. Then she pinched her nose to make her voice sound nasal.

"Hello, is Barbara Goldman there? . . . You are?"

She sounded as startled as I was. It was like getting a big fish on your line before you were ready to reel in.

"I'm looking for a Barbara Goldman who lived in New York sixteen years ago," Maggie improvised. "You didn't? . . . How about Brooklyn? . . . You've never been to Brooklyn? What about the Bronx?"

I heard a click and Maggie moaned, "She hung up!" Then she smiled. "It couldn't be your mother. She wouldn't do a thing like that."

She dialed another Barbara. This time she used a southern accent.

"Ah'm looking for ma deah friend Barbara Goldman who lived in New York sixteen years ago. . . . What's that? You've been living there for eighty-six years? . . . Sorry ma deah, ah've got the wrong numba."

She put the receiver down and fanned herself with her hand like a southern belle. "How'd ah do?"

"You-all were *totally* great."

"Want to try one?"

"No, ah just couldn't." I was trying to keep it light.

No one answered Maggie's third call.

"We ought to wait till later," I said. "People are at work now."

"She's probably home with three kids," Maggie argued.

"I thought she was a feminist."

"You can be liberated and still have children," Maggie said. "I plan to have at least five," she added, forgetting that the week before she wasn't planning on having any.

The next Barbara Goldman was very yakety. She'd only been in Manhattan ten years. No, she'd never lived in Brooklyn, but she had a cousin who did. Her cousin's name was Betty. Was it possible that we wanted Betty, not Barbara? Betty was a common name, but then so was Barbara. She liked Betty better. Maggie had to convince her that we didn't want Betty. She hung up exhausted.

"You do a few now," she said. "I've got to take this crummy polish off my nails."

"I can't!" I said vehemently. "With my luck I'd get her right on the phone, and then what would I do?"

"You'd say, 'Hi, Mommy, this is Baby.'"

"Maggie, you're too much!"

"That's what Lisa says."

"I've got to go home. Mom will be suspicious if I'm late for dinner."

"Suspicious of what? You really think she's going to say, 'Lori's not here for dinner. She must be out looking for her real mother'?" She picked up the phone again. "One more. I'll try Brooklyn this time. Maybe she's there, after all."

"She's not home!" A man roared over the phone so loudly even I could hear. "What do you want her for?" Maggie had to hold the receiver away from her ear.

"I'm a friend of hers from school," she replied in a screechy voice. "I'd like to talk to her."

"What school? The only one she ever went to was the school of hard knocks."

"Grammar school," Maggie said, thinking fast. "I'm an *old* friend."

"You don't sound so old to me."

"Is she there?"

"I'll take the message."

"I have to talk to her directly. It's *very important*."

"She in some kind of trouble again? Somethin' you don't want me to know?"

"Do you know when she'll be in?"

"If I knew, would I be askin' you what you know?"

"Thanks. I'll call again."

Maggie put the receiver down like it was about to explode. "There must be easier ways to find your mother," she said. "We ought to try Lisa's astrologer."

I felt like calling it quits right then. I didn't have to have my astrological chart read to know that my moon was not in ascendance that day. I'm a Gemini, and we're always going in too many directions at once.

After dinner, as I was heading out the door, Dad called, "Where to this time?"

"I'm just going over to Sue's," I mumbled.

"It seems you're always going over to the O'Brians'. You might as well pack and move over there."

Dad and Mom were sitting in the den, as usual, after dinner. He had some work spread out on the table and I was surprised he'd noticed me. He has this ability to concentrate completely on what he's doing, no matter what's happening around him. Maybe he had to train himself to tune out because Mike was always making something happen.

"Sue's helping me with Spanish," I lied.

"I didn't know Sue still remembered Spanish," my mother chimed in absently.

"She got her best grades in Spanish," I said quickly.

"I could believe that of Tony," my mother continued, as if to hold me there a little longer. "He's a real student. But Sue, well, she just seems too involved with animals to still have Spanish in her head."

"Mom, the two aren't related," I said. This conversation was getting idiotic. "I'll be back soon," I added, and fled out the door before anyone could remember that Sue had dropped Spanish in her sophomore year because she was almost flunking.

I nodded to Mr. O'Brian, who was watching TV in the living room, and went quickly into the dining room where Tony was studying.

"Did the letter from Ms. Barnes come?" Sue asked. This had become our regular greeting.

"No."

I must have sounded really low, because Tony commented without even looking up from his book, "It takes time. Be patient."

"Maybe she's not writing because she doesn't want to tell me anything."

"She'll write, but she may not say much," Tony said. "Some agencies are willing to reveal a lot more than others."

"Tony, you really have been doing research, haven't you?" Sue said, her eyes shining with admiration.

"That's not all I've learned," he said, closing his book and leaning back in his chair. "I'll bet neither of you knows why Lori's real parents aren't written on her birth certificate."

"Why?" Sue and I both asked at the same time.

"Because when a baby is placed for adoption, the original birth certificate is sealed, and another one is issued with the adoptive parents' names on it. As if they're the real parents."

"That's not right," Sue exclaimed.

"It may not be right, but it's the law."

It was strange to hear Tony explaining things like this, and to think that the baby he was talking about was *me*. You would have thought it was Sue, for all the questions she was asking.

"But why do they do that?"

"A number of reasons. They want it to seem as if the baby really belongs to the adoptive family. They also want to prevent the mother from coming back and claiming the child. And I guess they don't want the child to know who the real parents are."

It made sense. I knew I wasn't supposed to know where I came from. Otherwise, Mom and Dad and all their friends would have been willing to talk about it. My aunts and uncles never mentioned it when they came to visit from Chicago. Everyone acted as if I'd been born into the family. But it still gave me an uncomfortable feeling to know that my birth certificate had been rewritten. It was like rewriting history —something Mr. Innskeep would not approve of.

"I think adopted people must be the only group forced to have fraudulent birth certificates," Tony added. He sounded a little angry now, not impartial, the way he had before. "The more I think about it, the more I feel it should be unconstitutional to tamper with a citizen's birth certificate. I'm going to ask my professor about that."

"Oh, please do," Sue said, as if Tony's asking was going to change everything.

All this would have been enough for one day, but as Sue and Tony were walking me to the door, an incredible thing happened. If I read it in a novel, I wouldn't believe it. It would seem too much of a coincidence. But now I know that life really is stranger than fiction.

We were passing through the living room, where Mr. O'Brian had fallen asleep with the TV on. An announcer was saying, "Stay tuned to this station for our dramatic special, 'Which One Is My Mother?'—the story of an adopted girl who searches for the woman who gave birth to her."

Mr. O'Brian woke with a start, as if he sensed our presence, and jumped to turn off the set.

"No, leave it on," Sue said.

"Okay, I'll just go on up to bed then," he said with a yawn. "Must have been asleep already. Close up the place when you're finished, hear?"

I just stood there numbly until he left, and then I sank to the floor to watch the show. It was as if I was seeing the story of my life. There was this young girl, about my age, explaining to her adoptive parents that she wanted to find her real mother. They were very understanding, even bought her a plane ticket to Texas. When she got there, she looked up a group of adoptees called Operation Identity. They helped her find three women who had the same name as her mother. She went to see each of them.

The first was an unmarried woman running for a political office. She pretended not to know what the girl was talking about, and you could tell she was nervous about ruining her career. The second was a housewife with a few kids. She was very friendly, even looked something like the girl, but denied that she could be her mother. You had the feeling she was hiding something. The third was a woman in a mental hospital who admitted she was the mother. But she was so crazy you were supposed to wonder if she was just making it up.

The show left it all deliberately vague, but you got the message that the crazy one was probably the mother because she admitted it. I really felt sorry for the girl. She flew back to her adoptive parents and told them, "You are my only *real* parents. Those three women were all strangers." And then the commercials came on and you were supposed to believe that her curiosity was satisfied and she lived happily ever after washing her undies in Ivory Snow.

It was a real downer for me. The show seemed to be saying that you didn't have to bother searching because you'd only find a stranger—a crazy one at that. And I just didn't believe it. How could your mother be a stranger? No matter who she was, she was the one who brought you into the world. Whatever the name for her, it couldn't be "stranger."

When the commercials came on, I didn't say anything to Sue and Tony. I raced out of the house before they could turn on the lights and see the tears rolling down my cheeks. I fled across the lawn and got up to my room without Mom and Dad hearing me. I don't know how long I sat on the floor in the dark holding Winkie, who was so pleased at all the attention he didn't mind the big wet spots I was making on his fur.

I guess I was really terrified that my mother might be like those women on the show. Cold or crazy or something. I wanted to believe she would open her arms to me and welcome me back. But why had she given me up?

When I thought like this, my head would get all mixed up again. Even though I had imagined my parents as royalty and movie stars, a part of me couldn't imagine any other parents but the ones I had. What would happen if my fantasies turned into reality?

I never used to cry, but now I was crying all the time. It wasn't that I was unhappy, that was the weird thing about it. The tears seemed to come from somewhere else—someplace I didn't even know about. Someplace that my real mom and dad must occupy.

But I still didn't know if I was weeping for them—or for me.

eleven

The letter from the Rocking Cradle agency arrived a few days later. It was waiting on the hall table when we stopped by Maggie's house after school. We took it up to her room and locked the door. My hands were shaking so much that Maggie had to help me tear the envelope open.

The letter wasn't any longer than the one Maggie had written. It said:

Dear Miss Elkins,

I received your letter and would be willing to speak with you. I may not have too much information, but I will try to help you in any way I can.

Please call my office for an appointment on any weekday at your convenience.

Sincerely yours,

It was signed Sylvia Barnes.

I kept reading it over and over, hoping to discover something I hadn't seen before. It was like a message from outer space. Like it was from my parents themselves. This woman might even know them. She was a link. . . . But would she disapprove of my coming to see her without Mom and Dad's permission? Would she call them behind my back?

"Should I admit to her that my folks don't know about this?" I asked Maggie.

"Definitely not," she replied. "It's none of her business."

All the next day I was aware of that letter burning a hole in my bookbag. I didn't want to leave it at home for fear Mom might discover it. I was examining it once again in math.

I sent a note over to Maggie by way of Stephanie, who was sitting between us:

Mama Mag,

When should I see her? Spring vacation?

The message came back:

Too late. This is only the beginning of March. Go as soon as possible. Strike while the cradle is hot.

To which I replied:

I can't skip school.

Maggie's reply, "Why not?" had a message from Stephanie on it:

You two are totally obnoxious. I can't get my equations done. Bug off.

We continued plotting on our way to the next class. "Cut a Wednesday afternoon," Maggie said.

"Why Wednesday?"

"It's a matinee day, dum-dum. Tell your folks you have to see a show as part of your research for English or history or whatever."

"Maggie, you're a genius."

And she was. Our English class took a theater trip last semester, so it wouldn't seem odd that we were taking another one now.

"Make it a week from this Wednesday," said Maggie. "Call when you get home from school."

"I can't call from home. Mom might recognize the number on the phone bill."

"Clever thinking," Maggie admitted. "We'll have to do the dark deed here before rehearsal."

After school we went up to the second floor to use the public phone that was tucked away outside the art room.

" 'O! that this too too solid flesh would melt,' " I was thinking. But I merely said, "I don't have a dime."

"It's long distance, Baby," Maggie said, digging some change out of her wallet. "You'll need more than a dime."

"The whole United States treasury won't help," I said, leaning against the wall. "I feel like I'm going to faint."

"Stop being melodramatic," Maggie said. "Move over. I'll do it."

"But you can't say you're me."

"It's no big deal, dum-dum. I'm just going to get a secretary. Ms. Barnes is probably too busy diapering babies and giving them away to come to the phone."

The number was on the letterhead. Maggie used her most dignified voice with the secretary. She sounded like a debutante making arrangements for a ball. It worked. Fortunately, Ms. Barnes was free at three o'clock that next Wednesday. Unfortunately, I felt like I was going to throw up.

One part of me wanted to forget the whole thing. I'd hang my adopted parents on my family tree and be done with it. But another part of me, the part that had let Maggie write the letter and make the call, knew that I could never forget. Now that I had come this far, I couldn't turn back. It was too late. I could only go forward into whatever dark woods lay ahead.

"Don't worry, I'll go with you," Maggie said. I guess she could tell I wasn't faking—that I was really scared.

"I can't take you with me," I said tragically. "Ms. Barnes won't tell me anything if she thinks I'm still a baby. I have to grow up, don't I?"

This last was a question to which I hoped Maggie would answer, "No, you don't."

But even Maggie seemed to know that I did.

"Duck into the bathroom with me," she said. "I want to floss up before seeing Jack."

twelve

Strange things were happening in history.

As Mr. Innskeep's "family explorers" uncovered more and more family secrets, they became less and less eager to be called on. It didn't help to have Mr. Innskeep urging us on with the words of such wits as George Bernard Shaw: "If you cannot get rid of the family skeleton, you may as well make it dance."

We were in no mood for dancing with our skeletons in class. And to make things worse, Mr. Innskeep had everything completely organized now: we were to give short oral reports based on the written ones which were due at the end of the term. At the end of each period, he announced the names of those he was going to call on the next time.

When it was Maggie's turn, she was deliberately absent. She still hadn't decided what she was going to do about her father—use Alan in his place, or try to find out what she could from Lisa.

Maggie wasn't the only one in a state of panic. The day she and Howie were scheduled to speak, neither of them showed up. The following session, half of the class was missing —those who were supposed to speak, and those who were afraid they'd be called on if the other kids didn't show up.

Mr. Innskeep may be a little vague at times, but he's no fool. When he noticed that things were "rotten in the state of Denmark" (as he put it), he suddenly changed tactics and began to call on kids without warning. I had, of course, planned to stay home when my turn came—even if it meant faking an eight-week bout of mononucleosis—but there I was, trapped, when I heard those dreaded words: "Lori Elkins, would you please come forward." I sat there paralyzed from the ears down.

"Lori Elkins," Mr. Innskeep repeated. There was a trace of glee in his voice as he realized his scheme had worked. He had snared his first quarry—me.

Walking to the front of that class was like climbing Mount Everest. I was even panting for breath when I started to talk. I didn't know what I was going to say. I heard my voice speaking as if it had nothing to do with me, and then I listened to it along with the rest of the class.

"The project is not easy for me," my voice said, "because . . . because, you see . . . my mother and father . . . were orphans."

I paused, waiting for this to sink in, and for my next inspiration to come.

"That's incredible," said Mr. Innskeep, so flushed with excitement at this exotic bit of news that he forgot that I'd said my parents were visiting my grandfather last time. And so had I. If any of the kids remembered, they didn't let on—everyone knew that sooner or later their heads would be on the chopping block too.

"Is it something they don't like to talk about?" Mr. Innskeep asked delicately.

"Yes," I replied, tempted to add that I didn't like to talk about it either.

"How did they happen to meet?" He was hardly able to hide his curiosity.

"They grew up in the same orphanage," I said carefully, as if I were sliding on thin ice and if I made one wrong move I'd drown. "They fell in love—and married—in the orphanage."

"An orphanage wedding," Mr. Innskeep said, sounding totally intrigued. "Did they describe it to you?"

"It was a big wedding," my voice said, "because . . . because it was a big orphanage. All the friends they had grown up with were their bridesmaids and ushers."

What I was saying was not really so far out. My parents

—my real ones—were orphans in a way. They were lost somewhere out in the world—lost to me, at least.

"And they didn't know anything about either of their parents?"

"I think two of them were killed in car crashes and two in —in an earthquake, but I never ask. It makes them sad to talk about it."

"Well, this is an unusual situation," said Mr. Innskeep, clearing his throat the way he does when he is speechless. But I wasn't going to get off the hook completely.

"Maybe we can think of some variation on this project for you, Lori," he said. "You might want to look into the history of orphanages in this country. For that matter, the history of childhood would be fascinating. It's becoming a new field in itself."

"Where would I find the books?" I asked.

"There might be something on child welfare in our library. And I have some books on childhood through the ages at home. I know you'll make something creative out of the material. You always write good papers."

He added this last sentence like a pat on the head you'd give an orphan child.

It may have been my imagination, but I had the definite feeling that everyone was avoiding me on the way out of class. They seemed careful not to brush my clothes accidentally. As if I had the plague or something. Either they knew I was lying and they didn't want to show it, or they had swallowed the story whole.

Maggie, always the actress, played her role magnificently. She put her arm over my shoulder and walked solemnly out of the room with me, to our lockers.

It wasn't until we got to the auditorium that we could explode with laughter over the way I'd pulled things off in class.

"Why, Emily Webb, I do believe you are the cleverest child alive," said Maggie, while we were setting up for rehearsal. "Now let's get started on those string beans."

"Mama, I made a speech in class today and I was very good," I said. This was really one of Emily's lines.

"You must recite it to your father at supper," shrieked Maggie, delighted at how well the play fit our situation.

"Aren't you going to ask what it was about?" I said, stealing a line from Maggie—Miss Lathem would call it dramatic license. "I talked about orphans, Mama, and I fooled everyone."

"Well all my children are clever and you're no exception," said Maggie.

"Mama, will you answer me a question, serious?" I went back to Emily's lines. "Mama, am I good looking?"

"Why, Emily Webb, you're the ugliest critter I ever did see! You don't look like none of us, and that's a fact!" exclaimed Maggie, cracking up again, just as Miss Lathem, our drama coach, came in. Miss Lathem was once a famous actress, but now her face is as gray as her hair. She is always telling us to "modulate" and "project."

"I don't believe I remember that line, Maggie," she said, projecting her well-modulated voice effortlessly through the auditorium. "Are you trying to improve upon Thornton Wilder?"

"Not a chance," Maggie said. "I'm just shaking Emily Webb's family tree."

thirteen

Mom didn't say anything when I said I'd be home late that Wednesday because the class was going in to New York to see a matinee. It isn't really such a big deal. New York may be far from our town in one way, in that our lives are mostly centered on Southhaven, but some people commute to the Big Apple (as it's called) every day. And my parents often drive to New York on Saturday to go to dinner and the theater.

Dad gave me some extra money for the trip. "Stay with the class," he warned me. "No walking around the block alone."

My folks like New York a lot, but the papers are always full of terrible things that happen there. You can be walking along the street minding your own business, and wham, someone hits you over the head and grabs your purse. You can get stabbed if you don't hand everything over fast enough. But even here in Southhaven we have to be careful walking around at night. . . .

I was hoping no one would see me down at the train station. A lot of snow had fallen the night before and the wind was really sharp. I wrapped my scarf around my neck all the way up to my nose until just my eyes were showing. I felt like one of those Arab women you see in movies.

The train was almost empty, so I had my choice of seats. Some choice. The windows were so filthy you could hardly see out of them. Not that it really mattered, since there were only factories and slums flashing by, except when the Atlantic shore came into view. Once we started moving, the cars rattled so much that I couldn't read. I understood why Dad always complains whenever he has to take the train in to New York on business.

"The richest country in the world," he says, "and we can't have a decent railroad system for our people."

I sank into a lumpy seat and pulled the scarf tighter around my neck. I had faked a note from my mother that I had to go in to New York to see a dentist about a wisdom tooth. I was behaving like Mike now, as if he were my blood brother and there were bad genes in both of us. But not only were we from different parents, we were also from different agencies.

Now I wondered if Mike ever thought about his parents. He didn't act like he did, but I remembered being shocked when he screamed at Mom, "You're not my real mother! You can't tell me what to do!"

I never would have dared to say such a thing. But Mike didn't get slapped or anything for it. Maybe that was worse than being punished, because he never said it again.

It was easier to think about Mike than about what was ahead of me. Like how I was going to live through this interview with Ms. Barnes. Chris had been to some college admissions interviews already, and he said they were pretty scary. He'd even worn a tie to one. But they couldn't be as bad as this. I mean, college interviews are just about where you're going to spend your next few years learning things. But this was going to be about my whole past and where I came from. I decided that if I survived this, nothing would ever scare me again.

I got off at Penn Station and took a taxi to the agency. I was half an hour early, but I didn't want to walk and get mugged. Not now. Not before I learned who I was. And besides, what would my folks think if they got a phone call from the police asking them to pick up my body in some alley—and it wasn't with the class?

The taxi driver was real nice—he could tell I was nervous. He told me he had a daughter about my age. But when he said, "Well, here we are," I couldn't believe him. I had expected a big sign, THE ROCKING CRADLE, over the doorway of a building that was a cross between a hospital and a reformatory. All I saw was the number seven over the doorway of what

looked like a private home on a posh street. I thought I'd made
a mistake about the address. I do things like that. I pulled the
letter out of my purse, but this was the right place—7 East
Sixty-fourth Street.

So I paid the driver, thanked him, gave him a quarter tip (I
hoped that was enough), and rang the bell next to the entrance.
There was a buzz, and I pushed the door open. Inside, the
woman at the desk didn't seem surprised when I asked for Ms.
Barnes. She told me to sit down in the waiting room.

There was no one around. The place was as quiet as a
morgue—like I was the only visitor they'd ever had. I
wondered if I had been waiting in this room as a baby
—waiting with my real mother. Waiting to be adopted.

Once again I went over the things that Tony had told me to
say. "I came here because I want to know what happened to
my real parents. Why they gave me up. And if they are still
living in New York. And if you have my father's name in your
records."

I kept wishing I had worn a skirt instead of my usual
jeans. . . . I had been afraid Mom would notice I was getting
dressed up more than usual for a class trip if I did. Maybe I
would have looked older, made a better impression. . . .

In about ten minutes, but what seemed like ten hours, the
woman at the desk told me to follow her. She led me down a
corridor with green carpeting to a room at the very end. The
door was open. A woman in a dark suit stood up as I walked
in.

"You must be Lori Elkins," she said, extending her hand.

I hate to shake hands with people because mine are usually
cold and clammy, which they were now. Hers was dry and
warm, and I grabbed mine away as soon as I could, without
jerking it, so she wouldn't notice how nervous I was.

"Sit down, Lori," she said, motioning me to the chair in
front of her desk.

She might have been about Mom's age, but that's where the
resemblance ended. She had gray hair pulled into a bun at the
back of her head, and dark eyes that looked out over a long,
pointed nose. Dad always says he never trusts people with
pointy noses, and I should have been warned. But she was

trying to be nice. Her eyes were completely focused on me, as if I were the most important person in the world. I sort of liked her. There was a manila folder on her desk. She folded her hands over it.

"How old are you, Lori?" she asked.

"Sixteen," I said, but sitting there in that chair then, I felt like six.

"And what grade are you in?"

"I'm a junior."

"You mean you are in your third year of high school?"

"That's right."

"And what are your favorite subjects?"

"English," I said. I was thinking, "This is nutty. It's like a college interview."

Ms. Barnes went on like that for some time, asking me questions about my life in Southhaven, what I wanted to do after graduation, and if I knew shorthand or typing. Now it was beginning to sound like a job interview.

But finally she must have gotten tired of all this beating around the bush. Her voice became formal again as she ran her fingers along the edges of the folder, and said, "And now, Lori, what can I do for you?"

I tried to remember all the things I was going to say, but I couldn't think of them. So I just blurted out, "I was wondering if you know why my parents gave me up." It sounded terrible even as I said it. I wanted to go through the floor.

"Didn't your adoptive parents tell you anything?" she asked.

I couldn't give her all the versions of what they'd told me over the years. Nothing was very clear in my head now anyway. So I just replied, "They said they were poor and couldn't keep me. That's all."

"That's all?"

"And that they were counselors at a summer camp."

She didn't react at all. I mean her face just stayed the same, her nose pointing at me. Then she opened the folder on her desk and started looking through it.

"I don't see anything here about camp counselors," she said, "but that doesn't mean anything. That was seventeen years ago, Lori, and not all the details were put down then."

"Did you know them?" I heard my voice coming out queerly, sort of cracked, as if it belonged to someone else.

"No, I'm sorry. You see, I've only been here the last nine years, and the woman who handled this has retired. But let me explain our policy to you. Our board of directors has just agreed that we can give nonidentifying information to adoptees like you when they come back to us."

I must have looked puzzled, because she backtracked now. "Until recently, I would not have been able to talk to you as I am doing today. It was not our practice to tell adoptees anything. Sometimes we didn't even give them appointments. Now we are more relaxed about adoptees coming in. We can understand that they are curious. But because we are licensed by the state, we feel we cannot give them any identifying information. Do you know what I mean by that?"

My expression must have told her that I wasn't following. Or that I was pretty dumb. "That means that we can now tell you everything we know about your parents except things that would reveal who and where they are."

I realized then that I should not tell her I knew my mother's name already.

"Could you just read me what you have in there?" I nodded at the folder. "Except for the names, of course."

"Well, not everything," she qualified, "but I can tell you something."

She looked at the folder as if she were some kind of English teacher about to discuss the subject for the day.

"It says here that your mother was very attractive," she said. "About nineteen. Finished one year of college. Interested in the arts. She came in with her mother."

"Not with my father?"

Again she looked through the folder. "I don't see any mention of your father here."

"Not even his name?"

"It's usually not on our records, Lori," she explained patiently, her nose pointed directly at me. "Many times the girls simply refuse to give the father's name."

I must have turned beet red, or purple, or maybe a light bulb lit up over my head. "I'm sorry, Lori," she said. "I thought you knew that most girls who give up their babies do it because they're not married."

"I knew it," I lied.

"But she must have loved you very much to find a wonderful home for you with your adoptive parents. It says here that you were a beautiful, healthy baby."

I tried to stop them, but the tears started welling up in my eyes. They trailed down my cheeks faster than I could brush them away with my hand.

Ms. Barnes took a box of Kleenex out of a lower drawer and pushed it across the desk at me. The tears were pouring out now.

She left the room then, maybe to give me time to pull myself together. I kept tearing Kleenex out of the box as if I could plug up everything with it, but still I was aware of that folder lying on the desk. I wished I had the courage to get up and read all the things in it. I didn't dare. Ms. Barnes came back in a few minutes, sat down, and put her hands over it the way she had done before.

"I'm sorry if I said anything to upset you," she began. "To be truthful, I've never been convinced that our new policy of speaking so openly to adoptees is a good one. Especially for a girl as young as you. There was a wisdom to sealing those records, cutting off the past so that people could go on with their lives and not look back."

"But everyone is born to someone and connected by roots to that family tree," I said, remembering Mr. Innskeep's words. I was feeling really grateful to him then.

"Once a baby is adopted, it belongs completely to its new family," she said. "It is no longer illegitimate. There is no reason for anyone to know what happened in the past."

"But I *want* to know," I sobbed, the tears starting to flow again.

"You think you do, but I'm not sure you can handle it. Most of the adoptees who come back to us with questions are much older."

"I'm old enough," I wailed through my Kleenex.

Now she took another tack.

"Lori, your biological mother knew what she was doing

when she gave you up. We promised her confidentiality, that we would never reveal her secret. She's gone on to a new life now. It wouldn't be fair to try to contact her. You could cause a lot of harm."

This only brought on another flood of tears.

"Lori, have you been to see a psychiatrist?" she asked.

I shook my head no. "My brother has."

"I think you should ask your parents to take you to one too. Talking to a doctor would help you understand why you want to know about your biological parents. You'll find out how unimportant it is. You're what you are because you were raised by your adoptive parents."

I didn't say anything. Just sat there sniffling and snorting like an idiot.

"I'm sure your adoptive parents love you very much and want to help you." She smiled as she said this, as if it was just love I was looking for.

I got up quickly, spilling soiled Kleenex all over the carpet as I did so. All I wanted to do was to get out of there. "Thank you," I mumbled, remembering that Mom always said to say thank you.

She ignored the Kleenex and put out her hand as if we had just concluded a business deal. "Don't hesitate to call me after you've had some psychological help, Lori," she said. "My door is always open to you."

I gave her my hand reluctantly—it was clammier than ever. And then I fled down the hall and into the street. I started walking now, real fast, in the direction of the train station. I wasn't thinking about muggers or anything like that. All I could think was that they weren't married. It was like hearing they were dead, or something. It wasn't even a *them*. It was a *her*, and she had been only three years older than I was now when she had me. She had shrunk from being a married woman, like Mom, to a teenager, like me. Getting pregnant, having a baby.

I was at Eighth Avenue and Forty-sixth Street now, almost to Penn Station, where I was going to catch a train. It was a real tough neighborhood in the theater district. Men in leather jackets and cowboy hats lounged against the buildings as if they were deciding between taking a bus and mugging some-one. There were a lot of movie theaters advertising sex films with big lurid photographs of half-naked women. I saw girls in tight satin slacks and ratty-looking fur jackets standing around in some of the doorways. They looked real cheap. Maybe my mother had looked like that. I could imagine her as a prostitute right here on this street. And my father approaching her.

FATHER: Hello, sweetheart.
MOTHER: How'd you know my name, handsome?
FATHER: Same way you knew mine. How about us spend-ing some time together?
MOTHER: Just what I was thinking. Come on upstairs with me.

I couldn't see her face—or his. They were just shadowy people, the kind you see in gangster movies. They were after just one thing, sex. And I was the result.

Somehow I made it down to Thirty-third Street and onto the next train, a local, back to Southhaven. Not only was the train filthy, it shook and rattled until my bones ached as badly as my head.

I couldn't believe what a fool I'd been. Actually swallowing all those lies about my real parents being good, poor folk. Everything seemed changed now. Including me. I was no longer that innocent girl who took a train in to New York earlier in the day in search of her father's name.

Now I knew why it wasn't on the adoption papers.

The statue of the Virgin Mary in Sue's yard flashed through my mind. How could I tell Sue, of all people, that my mother was not only not married, but was probably a prostitute? A hooker. A whore.

Even Maggie would be shocked if she knew.

fourteen

I never did tell Mom what show I supposedly saw on the "class trip." When she kept asking, I finally snapped, "Leave me alone. I don't want to talk about it."

I didn't say much to Sue and Tony. Since I couldn't admit to them that my parents hadn't been married, I left it kind of vague. I said that my father had disappeared, and that they didn't put the father's name on the birth records in those days.

"Disappeared!" exclaimed Sue. "Maybe he couldn't face her because they were so poor."

"Some men do take off for that reason," Tony agreed.

Then I felt awful, because deserting your wife and baby sounded even worse than not being married. But I just shrugged and didn't say anything more.

I did tell Maggie and at first she was actually impressed. "That means she must be a feminist after all," she said. "They used to have children without getting married even then."

"But they probably didn't give them up," I said.

That stopped her for a moment. But she didn't dwell on it because all she wanted to talk about was Jack. She was *really* in love this time, she told me (as if I hadn't heard that every year with a different guy) and was going to the swimming meet in Hartford with him that next weekend. Chris wanted me to ask my parents if I could go too, but I knew they wouldn't let me, since it meant staying overnight. And besides, I didn't feel like being with him. I needed time to be alone and just think about things. I didn't want to be with anyone.

"I'm all packed, ready to leave right after school," Maggie said that Friday. "Am I ever glad I've got my IUD, if you know what I mean."

This set me to wondering if they'd had IUD's in my mother's day. Or something. She obviously hadn't taken any precautions. I was the proof.

I was just an accident—that was what really got to me. It wasn't so much that I was illegitimate, though that hurt too, but that I had never been in the grand plan of things. I didn't belong anywhere. I had just fallen into the world, unwanted. By anyone. By *her*.

My mother was gradually becoming a real person. She was a girl, like me. I still couldn't imagine her as a woman, though I knew she must be one by now. Was she married? Did she have kids? If she did, I had real brothers and sisters. Did she ever think of me? Was she sorry that she gave me away? Would she want to see me?

"Of course your mother would want to see you," Sue said one evening when we were sitting in her kitchen. She'd called and said she was alone, and would I come over. And then we were talking about *it* again. "What mother wouldn't want to see her child?"

"But maybe she wants to forget," I said. "And if I knocked on her door, it would remind her."

"Maybe she never forgot," said Sue. "There are some things you just don't." Her voice broke a little, and she turned away. I knew she was thinking of Jim again. We both looked out at the white alabaster Virgin on the lawn, holding her baby. Would Mary have ever parted with the baby Jesus? Even if they threatened to kill her?

Sue looked at me. "Are you all right, Lori?" she asked. "You seem sort of low. And you haven't been over lately. It's almost as if you've been avoiding us."

"I'm fine," I said. But I really wasn't. I didn't want to do anything except sleep. I could hardly drag myself out of bed in the mornings, and sometimes my head got so heavy in class, I would start nodding. Once, in Spanish, Maggie had to poke me when Miss Pickerel asked me to conjugate some verbs.

"Stay with us, Lori," Miss Pickerel said, moving on to Bottomless Pit, who was waving his hand wildly.

He'd changed a lot since he told the class he was adopted. Now he was usually up on his lessons, and when he tried to be funny, everyone was laughing with him, not at him. There he was, beginning to pull it all together, while I was beginning to fall apart. Maybe I should have gotten up and blown my cover too. "I'm adopted, see. I'm a bastard. I don't know my father's name. And I don't care. So there!"

I didn't miss Chris at all when he was away at swimming meets. I was having trouble concentrating on anything, even the lines for my part in the play.

"Are you not feeling well?" Miss Lathem called to me one day in rehearsal after I'd missed three cues in a row.

"I'm all right," I mumbled into the dark auditorium where she was watching us.

"Keep up your energy, then. Remember—professionals project."

And then she told everyone, "Let's take it from the top again."

We were on the scene in which Emily has doubts about getting married so young.

"I never felt so alone in my whole life," I said.

"Louder, Lori, project even more!" Miss Lathem called from the back row.

I practically screamed my lines as Emily told her papa that she hated George and she'd rather be dead than marry him. Call it projecting, or whatever, but now I could really feel Emily's desperation as she cried out to her father for help.

Mr. Webb was played by Warren Hinkley, the senior class president. He was tall and thin and had thick glasses that made his eyeballs swim when he looked at you. But he was real popular because he could organize things so well. He was a little stiff as an actor, but not bad. And he reminded me of my own father when he said, "Sh—sh—Emily. Everything's all right." As if not talking about the problem might make it go away. But Emily couldn't be comforted.

"Don't you remember that you used to say—all the time —you used to say: That I was *your* little girl. There must be lots of places we can go to. I'll work for you. I could keep house."

Frankly, I never did believe that last speech. That Emily would want to run away with her father. But, again, how did I know how you felt when your father was really your father? Maybe you felt different. I loved Dad, but I'd never felt attracted to him the way Emily did to hers.

"Sh . . . You mustn't think of such things. . . ." Warren went on with his lines, telling Emily what a fine young man George was and how lucky she was to be marrying him.

I suffered for Emily with the next lines when her father tells George that he's giving his daughter away. I know those are just words in the wedding ceremony, but now the whole idea of giving a person away really struck me.

"I love you, Emily. I need you," said Jack as George.

"Project!" called Miss Lathem, bringing me back to the play. "And say it as if you mean it!"

"Pretend it's Maggie," I whispered.

"On come on." He squeezed my hand and blushed as he kept vowing his eternal love. Then we fell into each other's arms in mock passion.

"Cool it," hissed Maggie.

"Good," said Miss Lathem, coming to the front of the auditorium. "Now let's go back a few scenes and take it from Mrs. Webb calling Emily to help her string the beans for winter."

My life seemed to have come to a standstill on all fronts. It was like the quiet before a storm. I felt like a pressure cooker just before the lid pops off. Which is what happened the following Saturday night.

The swimming team had no meet that weekend, so Maggie had suggested that Chris and I go out with her and Jack. Chris thought this was a great idea, and I went along with it because I couldn't think of a good excuse to refuse. Stephanie was having some kids over to her house that night, but we decided to do something more exciting—like have a drink at the Cork and Brew. Maggie had been collecting fake ID's for just such occasions, because you can't get into Connecticut bars until you're eighteen. But everyone knew that the Cork and Brew didn't card much.

"Who are you going out with tonight?" Mom asked when she saw me getting ready.

"Who do you think?"

"Well, I don't know. You haven't been going out so much lately. Chris?"

"Wait and see."

It really bothered me that my parents always insisted that I be picked up at the house rather than letting me meet whomever I was going with at some central location. I'd told them a million times that our generation does things differently. We don't *date*, as they call it. We just hang out together. But they said anyone I *hung out* with had to *come in* and get me. Which meant not just honking the horn, but coming inside and talking with them. It was really a drag.

Chris, as usual, didn't seem to mind.

"How are you, Mr. Elkins?" I heard him ask politely, as if he really cared. "And you, Mrs. Elkins?"

"Very well," Mom said. "And how are your aunt and uncle?"

They don't know each other socially, but sometimes Mom has her watch fixed in Chris's uncle's jewelry shop.

"My aunt's arthritis is kicking up again—other than that, they're great," Chris said.

I walked down the stairs like a zombie and got into my coat without a word.

"Good night, Lori," my mother made a point of saying as I sailed past her.

"Night," I called, running down the path to the car.

Chris didn't say anything as he started the motor.

"You didn't tell me your aunt has arthritis," I said accusingly.

"You didn't ask," he replied.

He didn't seem to want to talk about them any more than he'd wanted to talk about his brother. But I couldn't have cared less just then. I was rummaging desperately through my purse to see if I'd remembered to take the fake ID Maggie had given me. I finally found it stuck between two dollar bills in my wallet. Chris didn't have to worry, because he was nineteen.

As it turned out, the bouncer at the Cork and Brew hardly glanced at my ID. It could have been a credit card. Maggie and Jack were watching from a booth, clearly amused. They knew how nervous I always am until I'm in.

"I love you, Emily. I need you," Jack declared histrionically as he got up to make room for us.

"Put more expression in it. Like you mean it," coached Maggie. "And above all, project!"

"I love you, Emily. I need you!"

"I'm jealous," said Maggie.

"Stop competing with your own daughter," said Jack. "I know your type."

"Leave one of them for me," said Chris, moving closer against my side.

Usually we all had beer, but tonight we decided on gin and tonics. They laughed when I gulped mine down in a few swallows. I wasn't even aware that I'd done it. Usually I sip one drink all night. I don't like beer too much, and I hate the fuzzy feeling I get when I've had even one. But that night I wanted to feel fuzzy—zonked out—and I asked Chris to order me another gin and tonic.

When I wanted a third, Chris asked, "What's with you, Lori?" both in surprise and admiration. "Got a wooden leg?" He could drink all he wanted and never show it. But I couldn't, and I was obviously showing it.

"I want another one," I demanded, rattling the ice in my glass. And when Chris didn't signal the waiter immediately, I said, "I'll pay for it."

Maggie squealed, "Listen to her, she's so out of it she wants to pay."

She was referring to the fact that Chris always insisted on paying for everything when we went out, even though Maggie felt strongly that girls should pay their own way. And she usually did. It was part of the women's lib attitude that her mother had instilled in her: "Women should be independent," Lisa said. "They should have professions just like men. They should open their own doors, and be able to support themselves." But Lisa only did volunteer work, like her antinuke activities, and I noticed Alan opening doors for her more than once. Maybe she kept saying those things because she wanted Maggie to be stronger than she was.

Anyway, I always paid my own way when I was out with some guy who didn't have much money. But Chris said his old man was loaded—that's the way he put it—and now even Maggie was relaxing on this issue and letting Jack pay for movies, hamburgers, and things like that.

I guess I'd had about four drinks in rapid succession when Chris announced that we were leaving. I accused him of not wanting me to have any more. "I'm not leaving until I've had ten," I announced stubbornly. (At least that's what Maggie told me later.) I don't remember much except for Jack shouting, "I love you, Emily. I need you," and feeling that the ceiling was meeting the floor and that I'd bump into it if Chris didn't hold my arm more firmly.

I practically fell into the front seat of the car. I was still feeling good. "I like gin and tonics," I informed Chris as we drove along.

"I like you," was all he said.

"That's not the line, Chris," I screamed. "It's 'I love you, Emily. I need you.'"

"I love you, Lori. I need you," he said in a low voice, as if he really meant it. He wasn't kidding around the way Jack had been.

The radio was on and a rock group was singing about a lonely road and meeting lonely people on it. That really got to me, and I started singing along. I was on that lonely road, going nowhere, just like everyone else.

Chris parked the car in the same dark lane we'd discovered one night when we were just cruising around. He put his arm around me, as he always did, but this time he did it in a stronger, more protective way.

"It's been a long time, Princess," he said. That was his own secret name for me. "But you've overdone it tonight." He seemed concerned, as if he'd never been out with a girl who had downed four gin and tonics. But I knew he must have taken out girls who did worse things than that. Maggie was amazed that he was still putting up with me. I mean, with my *not* putting out. She was sure that once Chris tested this, he would disappear. But he was still around. "It must mean he's really gone on you," she had decided only the week before.

As I said, Chris hadn't even tried anything very much. Tonight, when he rested his hand on my breast, I wanted him to do more. I was hoping he would slide his hand all the way down my body. I didn't care what he did, as long as he held me close.

He seemed to know what I was thinking, as if my body were talking to his body, independent of words.

"Let's go in the back seat," he said. He opened the door on his side of the car and helped me into the back. I let him take off my coat, then unbutton my blouse and unhook my bra. Even in my knocked-out state I could tell he was really experienced at it. Then he took off his coat and shirt and we just lay there on the seat, holding each other and kissing, exploring each other's mouths with our tongues. "All I want is someone to make love to me," I kept thinking. That's what I had wanted Chris to do from the beginning, but I had never admitted it to myself—until now.

His hand started traveling further down my body, unfastened my jeans and slid through the space down to my hip. I wanted to fling all my clothes off, to do anything he wanted with him. This was my true nature coming out now. It was in my blood. This was the way my real mother would behave. Like mother, like daughter. Tears came to my eyes at the thought of her, and started sliding down my face into my mouth and his. And just when I thought he was going to do it, go all the way I mean, Chris sat up and started putting on his shirt.

"Get dressed," he said brusquely. He handed me my things.

I was stunned, and humiliated, and started putting on my bra mechanically. Everything I had been doing these days seemed mechanical.

"You're drunk, Princess," he said, playfully now, taking a loving nip at my nose and kissing each wet eye. "And you're going home before you get into trouble."

I didn't say anything all the way home. But at the door Chris pulled me to him and kissed me hard. I kissed him back, like I meant it, but nothing meant anything to me then.

I don't know how I got up to my room, but when I flicked on the light, I jumped, because there was Mom sitting at my desk, with Winkie at her feet. "Lori, I want to talk to you," she said.

It was two o'clock, later than I usually came in.

"Not tonight, Mom," I said, turning my back on her and pushing Winkie away.

"Where were you so late? I've been worried sick."

"At the Fiery Ox," I lied.

"Until this hour? And look at you, Lori. You're a mess. What have you been doing?"

My hair must have been all over my face, the way it is when I get up in the morning. But when you think about it, it was a dumb question, and I hated her at that moment: for being in my room when I wanted to be alone, and for giving me the third degree. Why didn't she say what she was really thinking—that I was a whore, just like my mother, doing what she would have done?

Mom had been a little edgy ever since she'd learned that Chris was older than the other kids. But now I understood that she wasn't worrying about Chris so much as about me—my bad blood. She could sense that it was starting to show itself. The way I had wanted all those gin and tonics was proof that blood will tell eventually. I had been holding my true nature back until now. I had been pretending to be so good when all I wanted was to drink and sleep around.

"I don't want to talk to you now," I said angrily.

"You never want to talk to me these days, Lori," she said very quietly. "I don't know you anymore."

"You've never known me!" I shouted, my voice rising uncontrollably.

"Be quiet. You'll wake Mike," she said. And, as an afterthought: "And Dad."

"I don't care if I wake the whole world! I won't talk to you!" I was screaming now as I ran down the hall and slammed the bathroom door behind me.

I looked at myself in the mirror. My eyes were red from the tears I had been shedding in the car, and there were dark shadows under them. They looked back at me the way they had all those years when I had been searching for my mother and father in them. But now those eyes were filled with grief.

I felt the floor rising to the ceiling again, the way it had at the Cork and Brew. I got the lid of the toilet up just in time. I don't know how many times I heaved. Finally I just settled on the floor, resting my cheek against the cold porcelain rim of the tub, wishing I could die. Though another part of me, the tragic actress, didn't want to die at all, and was enjoying her adult suffering. So this was what it was like to be grown up and to know *real* sorrow, not just the kind I'd read about in books and poems. " 'I'm going to meet you someday on that lonely road,' " kept going through my head. " 'And then we won't be lonely anymore.' "

I don't know how long I sat there like that, but when I came out my bed was turned down for me. And Mom was gone.

SECOND MEMORY

I am about four or five. I have a high fever and I have been throwing up. The doctor is standing with Mom over my bed. I am crying because he is going to give me a shot.

"Any special allergies in your family?" he asks.

"No," Mom says, "but there might be in hers. She's adopted."

"No medical history on her?"

"Nothing."

I throw up again, all over the bed. Mom carries me into the bathroom and holds my head over the toilet. Her cool hand feels firm on my forehead. Without it I feel I would disappear into nothingness.

fifteen

Chris gave me an Indian ring in the library on Monday during study period. He told me he had to measure my hand, and then he slipped it on my finger. It had a little turquoise stone set in silver. Having his ring didn't mean I was engaged to him, even though Maggie acted as if it did.

"You can visit him in college next year," she said. Chris and Jack were both waiting to hear where they got in. Their grades weren't so great, so they hadn't applied to the Ivy League schools. Chris wanted to go out to Colorado because of the skiing.

I didn't want any questions, so I didn't wear the ring at home. Mom hadn't said anything about that night I came in late. It was as if it had never happened. She and Dad were so preoccupied with Mike that they didn't seem to have any extra energy to worry about me. Which was lucky. I tried to make myself as scarce as possible, sleeping over at Maggie's a lot. And when I was home I'd bring my transistor radio down to the kitchen and play it loud while I was loading the dishwasher so Mom and I couldn't talk.

I wondered if I'd want to talk more to my real mother. I felt close to Mom and all that, but she really isn't my type. Like even though she and Dad go to the theater in New York, they seem to do it because it's the thing to do, not because it's something they need. And it's the same with books. Mom reads all the latest big fat novels, and Dad reads paperback mysteries and books about politics, but they never have literary discussions. Mom says she read writers like Virginia Woolf and Dostoevsky and Willa Cather when she was young, but it's like that's all over now—a phase she had to pass through before getting down to cooking and cleaning and the other realities of life.

But I wasn't being very literary these days either. I was listening to rock music a lot and writing lyrics.

This was my latest one: "Looking for You."

> Looking for you,
> That's all I do,
> In crowded streets, in every place
> That you might be.
> But I still don't know your face.
>
> Looking for you,
> Wondering where you might be,
> If you ever think of me,
> Ever long for that baby
> You once gave away.
>
> Looking for you,
> That's all I do,
> In every bus, on every train
> Where you might be.
> You sit across on every aisle,
>
> I find you in each stranger's smile,
> But inside I'm crying all the while.
> Looking for you.
> Looking for you.
> Looking for you.

I really cried when I wrote that one, but it made me feel better. Still, I don't think I would have done anything more about looking for my mother if there hadn't been this big article on adoption in *The New York Times*. Sue brought it over under her coat as if it were contraband and the federal authorities would confiscate it if they caught her.

She closed the door to my bedroom and spread the paper out on my bed.

"I just happened to come across this during lunch hour," she said excitedly, pointing to the headline over the article: SEARCH AND FIND GROUP WANT THEIR RECORDS OPEN.

The article was about a group of adoptees in New York City who met once a month to help one another search for their natural parents. There were quotes from a few of them who had found their mothers already and were now working to get the records open in New York.

There were also quotes from some adoptive parents who said that this group was not representative of the majority of adopted people, and that their children had no interest in searching.

The reporter did not take a stand. She ended the article by saying that just as there are some adopted people who want to know who their parents are, there are others who don't. But for those who did, she gave the address of Search and Find and the date and place of the next meeting.

"It's this Saturday," said Sue. "You really should look into it, Lori. Tony says it's hard to do anything without your father's name. Maybe this group will have some ideas about how to find it."

I was tempted to say, "I don't want to go any further. I want to stop right now."

When she saw me hesitating, Sue added, "I've got this Saturday off. I could go with you."

I was ready to say, "I couldn't care less if you're free. Leave me alone."

But I didn't.

Something in me knew that if I didn't act immediately, I might never act.

"I guess it wouldn't hurt to go," I heard myself saying.

sixteen

I told Mom and Dad that Sue wanted me to go in to New York with her to help pick up some things for the Easter holidays. The O'Brians usually have a big feast with the whole clan on Easter, so it all sounded natural enough.

The meeting was scheduled for two o'clock, which meant we had to take a late morning train. It was a good one, an express that didn't stop till we got to New York. We sat in the snack bar and ordered Cokes.

Sue was quiet for a while. Then she asked, "What's it like to be adopted?"

Her question took me by surprise.

"I never really thought about it until all this happened," she went on to explain. "Is it like losing someone you love?"

"It's different," I said slowly. I'd never tried to verbalize it until now. "It makes you feel like an outsider. As if you're not connected the way other people are to each other. As if something inside you is missing—like there's an empty space nothing can fill. Like you've never been born."

"It must really hurt," Sue said sympathetically.

"Not all the time," I said. "Usually you don't even think about it." I wanted to add, "But when you do, it's terrible. Like now." But I didn't. I felt ungrateful even saying these things to Sue. It was as if there were two me's: the good one, who seemed to have her act together, and the bad adopted one, who was just floating through life.

"I used to think I was adopted," Sue said.

"You did? Why?"

"I guess because I was so many years younger than my sisters. Mom said I was a gift of their later years. But I thought maybe they had gotten me from an orphanage or someplace like that."

"Sue, I can't believe it. You look just like your mom. I mean your face is the same shape and everything."

"I used to imagine that some wealthy couple had just dropped me off there, and was coming back to get me. I guess a lot of people must wish they were adopted at one time or another. It seems so romantic to think you really came from someplace else."

"It's hardly romantic when it happens to you," I said. I was quiet for a while, but since we were talking so honestly like this, I decided to tell her what was bothering me.

"Sue, I didn't tell you everything I learned at the agency." Pause. "My mother wasn't married."

"I thought so," she said softly.

"You did? Tony too?"

She nodded yes. "While he was doing his research, he discovered that most women give up their babies because they're not married. He told me that's why your father's name wasn't on the adoption papers."

"You don't hate me?"

"Hate you?" Sue squeezed my hand. "Lori, what difference does it make?"

"You pray to the Virgin Mary and all those priests come and have Sunday dinner with you. What would they think?"

"What do you think they hear in confession all the time? Catholics need confessional because they always have things to confess. Lots of girls get into trouble and the priests have to make arrangements for them to put the babies up for adoption."

I really felt good after Sue said that. I was even glad we were going to New York together.

The community center where the meeting was being held wasn't too far from Penn Station. In the lobby we saw the sign: SEARCH AND FIND—ROOM 417.

We took the elevator. It was crowded with kids going to the

gym, to crafts and music lessons. I wished I was little again and on my way to things like that. I felt a million years old, as if I had to do something now that was outside of ordinary life.

The meeting was just getting ready to start. The room was set up with rows of folding chairs, most of which were filled with women. The majority looked as if they were in their late twenties or thirties, but some of them were really old. There were just a few men. Sue and I slipped into the back row. We must have been the youngest ones there.

A woman named Claire Collins introduced herself as the founder of the group and welcomed everyone. She said she could see a lot of new faces and hoped she'd have a chance to talk to everyone personally. She was tall and as thin as a bean pole. She had dark hair and round horn-rimmed glasses that gave her face an owlish look. For the sake of the newcomers she told a little about herself—how she'd searched for her mother for eight years only to find that she had died the year before. She still didn't know who her father was, because her mother had gone to her grave with that secret.

"I wish I'd started searching earlier, instead of waiting until I was thirty-five," she said. "Just remember, only your birth mother can tell you who your father is. By waiting, I lost my chance to meet them both."

"Why did you wait?" someone up front asked.

"Okay, the usual reason," Claire replied. (She punctuated everything with "okay.") "I felt too guilty. I didn't want to hurt my adoptive parents and decided to wait until they were gone. But by that time, my birth mother was gone too."

A kind of collective sigh went through the room, as if we were all reacting as one.

"Okay, there was nothing I could do about my own situation, but I decided maybe my story could help others. I wrote a book that a lot of you have read: *Growing Up Adopted.* And then I started receiving hundreds of letters from adopted people. Thousands. And they were all asking the same questions: 'Who am I? Who are they? Why did they give me up? Will I hurt my adoptive parents if I look for them? How do I search? Does my birth mother want to be found? What happens after I find her? Should I search for my father?' "

I felt all choked up, as if I couldn't breathe. I had never heard anyone express exactly what I was feeling before. Claire Collins was putting all my thoughts into words. The questions I never dared ask.

Everyone was absolutely still as she spoke. She was like a guru giving us the word. Encouraging us to be brave. She made it sound like the most natural thing in the world to want to know where you came from.

"And then I started this group with some of the adoptees who had written me," she said. "Each one of our experiences is different, and yet the same. We have a search workshop at the end of each meeting to help our members with their individual problems." (Sue touched my arm when she heard this.) "But in this part of the program we ask a few members to tell where they are in their search or reunion. Because we've learned that the search doesn't end after you find your mother. In some ways, it's just the beginning."

"You can say that again," the man in front of me whispered to the woman next to him.

"Let me just add for the sake of our new members, that even though this group believes everyone has a right to search, no one says the search is easy. There are times when you feel you're climbing a steep mountain with no trail. Or you're on a roller coaster—lots of ups and downs. One day you're excited because you've found a new piece of information to fit into the puzzle, and the next you're in the dumps because you've hit another dead end."

"That's it," a woman up front agreed. "An emotional roller coaster."

"But you get to that final station one way or another," Claire said. "Now we're going to talk about what you do when you arrive and no one's there to meet you. Larry is going to tell you what happened after he found his mother."

"Found her and didn't find her," Larry said, getting up from a seat in the first row.

Larry must have been in his late thirties. His hairline was receding and he had a slight paunch. He looked ill at ease the way he kept adjusting his tie.

"First off, I never would have started searching if my wife, Ellen, hadn't insisted," he said, looking over at the front row.

"I wanted to know where our baby got his nose," Ellen said, half standing up.

This got a laugh from everyone.

"And his toes," she added.

Another laugh.

"But seriously," she added, "I wanted to know the missing part of our baby's background. But I'll let Larry tell it. He's the one who's adopted."

"I'll trade places with you," Larry said, much more relaxed now. "Well, let's see, Ellen found this group on her own and made me come. And it's the best thing that ever happened to me. Once I let myself think about it, I really wanted to know who my mother was. The search workshop suggested I look on my baptismal record, and I'll be darned if her name wasn't there."

"Almost to scare him to death," Ellen popped up, and then down once more.

Now Larry just stood there fingering his tie again, as if he was still scared.

"How did you approach her?" Claire asked encouragingly.

"I wrote her a very careful letter about myself, my wife, and my children," he said. "Ellen typed it. I wanted her to think I was respectable, not down and out, wanting something from her. But she didn't answer it. We waited a few months, and then Ellen insisted I call her."

"I figured he would have waited forever," Ellen said, popping up again briefly.

"So I called," Larry continued. "I got her at home the first try. It was after nine in the morning so I figured her husband would be at work and she could talk."

He paused to tighten his necktie here, as if he was really just about to speak to her.

"I told her I was adopted and thought she was my mother. She didn't like that. Said she didn't know what I was talking about. That I must have the wrong person. I said even so, I'd like to meet her just once, anyplace good for her. But she kept saying I was barking up the wrong tree, and things like that. Then she hung up."

"And what happened?" Claire asked, when he just stood there not saying anything.

"I tried to call the next week, but I couldn't get through. She'd changed her number and unlisted it."

"I say that proves she's the one," Ellen said, standing up again. "Otherwise, why all the fuss?"

There was a general stir in the room as everyone began talking at once, to Larry or to a neighbor. Some told how their mothers had refused to see them, too, and others offered advice on what to do in that situation.

I felt goose pimply all over. I couldn't imagine my mother not wanting to see me. But then I couldn't imagine my mother. She still didn't have a face. A few nights before, I dreamed I saw her from the back in a room full of people. But when I got up close, she wouldn't turn her head. I kept trying to see what she looked like, but I couldn't. Sometimes she'd be standing there all dressed up like some famous movie star, and other times she'd be in rags. And I kept thinking that if I could only see her face, then I'd know. . . .

Claire brought the meeting back to order after a while.

"Okay, Larry's mother isn't the only one who's tried to deny who she is. You've got to understand that she's been taken by surprise. She's probably kept it a secret until now, and she's terrified that Larry is going to blow her cover. She may even be glad to have heard from him, to know he's alive, but she's running scared. She'll need time to come around. Remember, she's been through a lot. Society makes it a very shameful thing to have a baby out of wedlock. There's a lot of guilt there too, about having given her baby up. And a lot of pain."

"Real pain," said a woman who announced that she was a birth mother as she stood up. "I'm searching for my son because I want him to know that I didn't want to give him up. I was just a confused kid. My boyfriend denied he was the father. My folks were on my neck. The social worker said the best thing I could do was give my baby to a married couple who could raise him better than me. I believed her. Signed him away. And I've been depressed ever since. Even been hospitalized a few times. I don't know if my son is dead or alive. He could have died as a baby, or in Vietnam. I'll never know, if I don't find him myself."

Some of the people in the room were crying and others were dabbing at their eyes. I felt all choked up. I noticed that Sue had her hands over her eyes.

"You'll find your son someday, Pat," Claire told her. She obviously knew her real well. Then she turned to the rest of us.

"It might be of interest to you newcomers that Pat is just one of the many birth mothers we have in our group."

"Why do you say '*birth*' mothers?" a woman asked. "Isn't the word 'natural' mothers?"

"Okay, we can't say 'natural' mothers, because adoptive parents object that it makes them sound *unnatural*. We don't want to say 'real' mothers, because even though birth mothers are the *real* ones in one way, in other ways they're not. And we object to adoptive parents using 'biological' because it sounds so unfeeling. So we're using '*birth*' mother as a compromise."

"Complicated," someone remarked.

"And silly," Claire said. "I don't think we should get hung up on side issues like names because there are more important battles to be fought—like getting the records open."

I was watching Pat, the birth mother, who had taken her seat near me. She had short brown hair streaked with gray, and wore no makeup. She was a little on the heavy side, but there was something attractive about her. She seemed like a warm, caring person. I wondered if my mother looked anything like her. If she had been depressed at giving me up.

"Life would be a lot easier if you were my mother, Pat," Larry said now, with a sheepish smile.

"I'd like to tell that mother of yours a few things," Pat answered. "What are you going to do next?"

"I'm going to write her another letter. And if she doesn't answer that, I may have to knock on her door. If I ever get up the nerve."

"I'll knock," said his wife. "I have a few things to say to her too."

"I hope you don't have to," said Claire. And to us: "We

don't like to barge into a mother's house, because we believe she has a right to privacy. Privacy, that is, from others, but not from her own child."

There was a murmur of agreement, and then Claire added, "Of course, some of you are going to find mothers who will fling open the door with joy. Mothers like Pat who have refused to live a lie, and have never forgotten their children. Tracey had that experience, and she's our next speaker. Thank you, Larry."

Larry gave a kind of bow and sat down as Tracey took his place in front. She was short and trim in a tailored suit, and probably in her twenties.

"I searched for my mother for two years and finally found her three weeks ago," she said excitedly. Everyone clapped. Sue and I smiled at each other. Tracey's happiness spread over the room like the sun coming out from behind clouds.

"We met in a hotel lobby and talked and talked. It was amazing. We have the same interests. We both love to bowl and to cook—and to talk."

This got a big laugh.

"Do you look like each other?" someone asked.

"I'd have known her anywhere. She has the same long, thin face, the same eyes. She's a little shorter, but we have the same gestures. We even hold our cigarettes the same way. She has three other children, and she's going to tell them about me."

"Did she tell you who your father was?" Claire asked.

"No, not yet. She didn't want to talk about him."

"That's typical," said Claire. "A lot of mothers don't want to talk about the man who caused them so much pain. They've tried to forget that part of it. Talking about him is like bringing him back into their lives."

I realized that I hadn't really imagined my father either. Never thought about him as a real person.

"Keep after her," Claire was saying. "You're doing fine, but get her to tell you who your father is. He's the other half of your family tree."

Sue gave me a poke and a wink.

"Mr. Innskeep should be here now," I whispered to her.

"This is a perfect time to hear from Amanda," Claire said. "She's just met her father."

Amanda, a tall, gangly woman whose left eye twitched, walked to the front.

"It took me over a year to get my mother to give me my father's name," she said. "I found him easy enough after that. Just looked in the phone book in their hometown. Got him at home in the evening. Boy, was he ever surprised to hear from me. He said I should write to him at the office. So I did. He wrote back saying that he'd be willing to meet with me on one of his business trips to New York. But he wasn't admitting anything then."

"How about when you met him?" Claire asked.

"That was something else," Amanda said, her eye twitching away. "We met at the bar of his hotel at lunchtime. He was really belting them down. Said my mother ran around with a lot of guys back then, so maybe he was my father, maybe he wasn't. Boy, he was lying like mad, because we look like two peas in a pod. Anyway, he relaxed when I told him I didn't want anything from him. He probably thought I wanted to clean him out. Told me he's got two sons. One just a little younger than me."

"Is he going to tell them about you?" a woman called out.

"I don't know. He left it kind of vague. I'd like to meet them. I was raised as an only child."

"Anybody here met their brothers or sisters?" Claire asked the group. A lot of hands went up. Claire chose a young woman who was jumping up and down. She had shortcropped blond hair and was very athletic looking.

"My half brother and I are almost exact look-alikes," she said. "Some people think we're twins. He starts a sentence and I finish it. He says if he had met me on a blind date, he would have married me. And I know I would have married him. Sometimes we even joke about incest."

"Some joke," said Claire. "Anybody else here with that experience?"

A number of people shouted yes.

"Sometimes an adoptee feels he or she has more in common with a brother or sister than with the parents," Claire said.

"They're closer in age, and they don't have all that past history complicating their relationship."

Claire looked up at the clock on the wall now. "Okay, we have just a few more minutes until the search workshop." And then she said to Amanda, who was still standing up there, "Have you told your adoptive parents about your search?"

Amanda's left eye started going like mad again. "I haven't told them anything," she said. "It would kill my adoptive mother to know I've found my other parents. She told me they were dead."

"It's too bad adoptive parents have to feel so threatened," Claire said. "If only they could understand that it really helps our relationship with them once we've solved who we are."

Now a young woman stood up and said she wanted to introduce her adoptive mother, who had agreed to come to the meeting.

"It wasn't easy for Mom when I told her I wanted to search," she told us. "But now she wants to help me. Stand up, Mom."

Her mother was clearly hesitant about getting up. She was thin and pale, while her daughter was round and ruddy. But they were holding hands and looked really close.

"To be honest, I'm not thrilled she's doing it," the mother said. "I don't want her to get hurt. But if it's what she wants, I'll go along with it. I'm with her all the way."

There was a big applause when she said this.

I tried to imagine my mom coming here with me and standing up like that, but I couldn't see it. Or Dad either.

Claire had some announcements to make after that. A lawyer was coming to the next meeting to advise everyone on how to go to court and petition for their records.

"We should bring Tony for that," Sue whispered.

"It's getting more complicated," Claire said. "Until recently you could get your records if you had a psychiatrist's letter or some other proof of 'good cause,' as it's called, to convince the judge that it was vital for you to know your background. But a lot of the states are making it more difficult now. In some you have to get the written permission of your adoptive parents *and* your birth parents."

"How can you get your birth parents' permission if they're the ones you're looking for?" a man asked.

"The court does the searching—at your expense," Claire said.

"It's always at our expense," a woman grumbled.

"That's right," Claire agreed. "And the birth parents have a right to refuse to see you. That's why our search workshop is so important. We don't have to ask anybody for anything if we can find our parents by ourselves—without an outside intermediary who may frighten them off."

She glanced at the clock again. "Okay, this is a good time to break. Those of you who need help can go into the search workshop now. The rest can join us at the punch table for refreshments and an informal get-together."

About half the people moved on to the next room, and Sue and I followed them. A portly man with a walrus mustache sat at the end of a long table and invited us to take chairs around it. He said he was a genealogist. I wished Mr. Innskeep could see me now, meeting a real genealogist. But I knew I wouldn't tell him about it.

As the last few people were meandering in, Claire entered the room and looked around. Then she crossed over to Sue and me.

"I don't think I know you," she said.

"I'm Lori Elkins," I said, jumping up. "And this is Sue O'Brian. She came with me, but she's not adopted."

"And are you?"

I nodded.

"How old are you?"

"Seventeen," I lied.

"You don't look even that old," she said. "Okay, I'm sorry, Lori, but no one under eighteen can attend these search workshops."

"Why not?" I felt myself flushing bright red as everyone turned to look at us.

"Okay, because you're still a minor. We'd love to help you, but we don't want to get into trouble. If your adoptive parents sued us, we could lose our room in the community center and even our tax-exempt status."

She went on listing the reasons, as if she needed more than one. I could tell she felt bad about it, but I had to leave.

"Come back next year and I promise to help you search myself," she said, guiding us to the door.

I said I would, but I knew I wouldn't. It wasn't that I was mad, or that I didn't understand. I was hurt. If they wanted to help adopted people, they should help everyone, no matter what their age. Kids are human too.

seventeen

"Don't take it so personally, Lori," Sue said when we were outside on the street.

I didn't say anything. Once again I felt really tired. I just wanted to go to sleep for a hundred years and not have to think about this anymore.

"We'll do it without them, you'll see," Sue continued. "Tony and I will help you find her."

I didn't know why I was so upset. It wasn't that I was even that eager to find my mother. It must have been that I had felt so comfortable with the members of that group. They made me feel that I wasn't evil or guilty for wanting to know about the past. I felt I really belonged with them—and then they rejected me. Told me I couldn't be one of them. I was still an outsider.

We were near Penn Station now. A sports event from Madison Square Garden must have just let out because a lot of people holding pennants were coming toward us from the other direction.

"All those adoptees found their mothers, so it couldn't be too hard. Tony will figure out the best way to do it," Sue's voice droned on in the background as we pushed our way through the crowd.

I became separated from her by some people crowded around one of the doorways. In trying to get by, I found myself almost face to face with a disheveled woman who was standing on the stoop tying up a bunch of tattered shopping bags with dirty string. She had on two unmatching tennis shoes with torn socks sagging down over both of them. A striped ski cap covered her head, and her hair stuck out in tangled clumps around her face. I knew that women like her are called "bag ladies." They live on the streets and go through garbage cans for their food. I had always wondered what terrible tragedies in their lives could reduce them to such an existence.

It was hard to tell the bag lady's age, but her face was kind of nice. She must have had a home once, been somebody's mother. And then I got this wild idea that she could be mine.

I imagined myself walking over to her and saying, "Mother?" And her pushing some hair out of her face and looking up:

BAG LADY:	Did someone call me?
ME:	It's me, Mother. Lori!
BAG LADY:	Lori? Am I dreaming? My lost baby?
ME:	I'm not lost anymore, Mother. I'm here.
BAG LADY:	If I'm dreaming, I don't want to wake up. My baby.
ME:	I've been looking for you, Mother.
BAG LADY:	And I've been looking everywhere for you, Baby. All these years, looking so hard.
ME:	But why are you just sitting here, Mother?
BAG LADY:	Got to sit somewhere, Baby. I fell on hard times after I gave you up.
ME:	But don't you have a home to go to?
BAG LADY:	The subway is my home. But I come up for air sometimes, like now.
ME:	What's in all those bags, Mother?
BAG LADY:	Dreams, Baby.
ME:	Dreams?
BAG LADY:	Old dreams of what was, and dreams of what might have been. I've been collecting them for years, tying them up tight for safekeeping.
ME:	I dreamt of you, Mother, all the time I was growing up.
BAG LADY:	Those dreams are probably in my bag too, Baby. You wouldn't have an extra piece of string on you, would you?
ME:	You don't have to tie up any more bags,

	Mother. I'm here now.
BAG LADY:	Oh, it's a habit, Baby. Wouldn't know what to do with myself otherwise.
ME:	You can come to Southhaven with me.
BAG LADY:	Where's that?
ME:	In Connecticut. It's a small town—but very nice. You can get cleaned up and have something to eat.
BAG LADY:	I could use something to eat. Don't get the chance too often. But you best run along now, Baby. I'm busy here.
ME:	You mean you won't come with me?
BAG LADY:	Never cared much for small-town dreams.
ME:	It's not too late for us, Mother.
BAG LADY:	That's the biggest dream of all, Baby. Here, stuff it over in this bag.

"Lori, I turned around and you weren't there. I thought I'd lost you." Sue was at my side. "What's going on here?"

"Nothing important. Just a bag lady."

"Let's hurry now," Sue said. "We'll miss the express train if we don't get a move on."

She grabbed my arm and we both started running. We had ten minutes to cover three blocks and find the right track. I didn't think we'd make it, but we jumped on the train just as it was ready to pull out. The doors closed behind us.

"What luck!" gasped Sue.

We fell panting into the two nearest seats.

"Have you ever talked to a bag lady?" I asked her.

"No, why?"

"No reason. I just wondered." I put my coat on the rack above us and sank into the seat again. "I feel like we've been gone for years."

"I know what you mean," Sue said with her eyes closed. "And I think I know what it's like to be adopted."

eighteen

It wasn't until we were on the bus home from the Southhaven station that we realized we had no packages to show we'd been shopping.

"We can say I had them all sent if your parents ask us," Sue said.

But it wasn't necessary. My house was ominously silent when I came in. It was the kind of silence that's filled with tension. That means something's wrong with Mike again. Winkie didn't even bother to jump up on me.

Mom and Dad were in the den, just sitting there. They couldn't have cared less about how my shopping had gone. Dad had a glass of Scotch in his hand, and Mom's eyes were red.

Mike had run away. He'd left a note that they shouldn't call the police. He just wanted to take off on his own for a while. He'd be all right.

"Where is he going to go—a thirteen-year-old kid?" Mom asked no one in particular.

"And probably not more than a few dollars in his pocket," Dad said.

"He'll be all right. He said so himself," I said, trying to reassure them. But I wasn't so sure myself. Again I realized how Mike had the power to make them suffer, some special talent for pushing the pain button. A part of me wanted to find him and shake him hard, but another part understood for the first time that he might be suffering too. He was just expressing it in his own way.

I couldn't stand staying in the room with them, so I gave Dad a kiss on his bald spot, and patted Mom's arm, and went upstairs. I don't know how long they sat there like that, because I went to bed early. But I knew they were reaching the breaking point.

Things broke sooner than I expected.

It must have been two in the morning when I was aware that the phone was ringing in the hall. I sat up in bed and heard Dad talking in the hoarse voice he has when he first wakes up. The call was from the police. Mike had just been caught trying to set fire to a country club on the outskirts of town. He hadn't lit the blaze yet, but the night watchman had caught him soaking some rags in oil. They had him at the police station now. Dad should come right down.

Mike in jail. It was too much. Mom wanted to go with Dad, but he insisted that we both go back to sleep.

As if we could.

"Will you be able to get him out?" Mom asked.

"Don't count on it," Dad said. And this time he wasn't kidding.

Dad was gone for the rest of the night. I couldn't sleep. I kept thinking of the strangest things. Like the time Mike brought Mom a bouquet of roses, which really surprised her because roses are expensive. But when she was out of the room, Mike told me the florist had given them to him free because it was the last day of their bloom. The next day they would be dead.

I couldn't believe it. The roses seemed so fresh and alive. But the next morning when I came downstairs, they were all drooping in the vase, as if someone had broken their necks in the night.

Mike was like those flowers, I thought. He seemed so alive, so full of energy, but something inside him had been dying. And then it suddenly collapsed. Maybe he was setting fire to the world that had somehow misplaced him. Maybe he was saying, "Hey, everybody, look at me. You thought you could throw me away, but you can't get away with it!"

I guess I must have dozed off around dawn. When I came down in the morning, Dad was sitting with Mom, telling her what happened. He had managed to get his lawyer and Mike's shrink to come down to the station. They'd been able to arrange for the charges to be dropped—since there was no actual fire—if Mike were sent to a place for psychiatric treatment.

"It may only be for a few weeks," Dad said. "The doctor just wants to quiet him down and try to learn what's going on."

The hospital (they call it a residential treatment center) was in western Connecticut, about two hours from our house. It was mainly for teenage kids who had freaked out on drugs or had more than the usual problems. Mom and Dad were told that eventually they could visit once a week, but to wait a while. The shrink advised them to take a vacation or just relax. Everything possible was being done for Mike. All he needed was time.

I couldn't help but feel guilty. I should have talked to Mike more, shared what I was doing. Maybe it would have helped him to know I was having problems too. But now he was in his own lonely space and I had lost the power to reach him. Maybe if he had been my own blood brother we would have been closer. I didn't know.

There were a lot of things I didn't know then that I know now. I thought I had a choice about what I was going to do about my own life. I thought I could just forget about that Search and Find meeting—even forget about searching for a while. I became the model daughter at home, to make up for Mike's absence. I talked to Mom over the dishes, told her about rehearsals; I even let Dad test me on my lines. When their friends dropped by in the evenings that next week to cheer them up, I sat around with them as if I was interested in what they were saying. They'd start with world affairs, and go on to things that were happening in the community, but the conversation would always come around to the problems of raising kids. Especially teenagers. Still, other people's troubles seemed nothing compared to ours now that Mike had been sent away. And that was strange, because until then our family had seemed so normal and together compared to a lot of others

—where the parents were either getting divorced or cracking up.

I wondered if my folks felt particularly embarrassed with people who knew that Mike wasn't really their son—if they felt like failures. I wanted to tell them that Mike would probably have been impossible with his own parents too.

Or would he? I had to think about this, try to understand.

In the meantime, I kept jumping up like the perfect daughter, pouring coffee, getting plates for cake, and answering politely whenever anyone spoke to me. I felt as if I was defending the family name.

When Sue called to tell me Tony had some ideas about finding Barbara Goldman, I told her I couldn't do anything more about my search now because of Mike. That I wasn't even going to think about it. And I thought I wasn't. But of course that was dumb. Because once you've started thinking about where you come from, I mean really thinking about it, you're a goner. I could no more stop thinking about my mother and how I wanted to know more about her than I could stop getting up in the morning and going to school, and doing all the things I did.

It was as if I was on one of those airport escalators that moves you from one end of the terminal to the other, even though you stand in the same spot.

nineteen

Mr. Innskeep used to tell us that history is a lot like theater. That it gradually works itself up into some kind of crisis that has to be solved, and then there is some sort of resolution.

That's what was happening in our history class. It was a real crisis when the kids realized that they couldn't get out of those oral reports, but then they kind of relaxed and let it all hang out. And the result was they began to see each other as real people with parents and problems and weaknesses the same as everyone else's. They got the message that it was safe to drop their masks and act natural with each other.

The Friday that Hortense and Artie Potter leveled with us and with themselves was the turning point for us all.

I would never again think Hortense was all bad just because she bragged that her ancestors had come over on the *Mayflower*. I realized this was something she hid behind to make herself seem more important. She must have been really insecure about herself because she was kind of weird looking —as Stephanie would say, she was "totally" skinny on top and "totally" fat on the bottom.

Now she was totally honest with us when she talked about the Pilgrims.

"They really suffered on that trip," she said. "The *Mayflower* was hardly a modern oceanliner with shuffleboard and deck tennis. They spent sixty-six terrible days on that small boat with hardly any food or water, and not enough room to move around. And there wasn't a Howard Johnson Motor Lodge and restaurant waiting for them when they landed in the freezing winter winds. Just wilderness."

Hortense found out from a great-aunt that one of their illustrious ancestors had been killed in a drunken brawl, and his grandson had been imprisoned for some kind of land fraud.

"I guess coming over on the *Mayflower* didn't make them or their children better people, or me either," she said. "Or happier. I think if they'd had a choice they would have chosen to come later in more comfort. I've been acting like a snob about all this, and there's nothing to be snobby about. They were just ordinary people like everyone else."

We spontaneously burst into applause as she sat down. We knew it wasn't easy for her to admit all those things, and we wanted her to know we appreciated it.

After Hortense, Artie got up and said right off that a black family tree isn't even good for kindling wood.

The class was so stunned you could have heard a paper clip drop. Artie never talked about being black, and of course we never mentioned it. Most of the time we forgot it ourselves because he seemed so much like us. We didn't even give it a thought that he was always cleaner and more neatly dressed than the other guys. Sometimes he even came to school in a sports jacket and a tie. But now I noticed that his shirt was really wrinkled and he was wearing blue jeans for the first time. He didn't seem like the Artie we knew. Even his way of speaking was different.

"My family been in this country hundreds of years, long before most of yours got here," he said, deliberately using jive talk. "We should be top dog by now, man, but we're still at the bottom of the barrel. My older brother's been in the slammer three times already in New York because he says he's gonna take what Whitey owes us. He says he's not gonna take any more shit, man."

Mr. Innskeep looked really startled. He didn't interrupt the way he usually does when any of us uses a swear word.

"My ma, she works her fingers to the bone cooking and cleaning house for Whitey," Artie continued. "Then she comes home and stays up all night doing our laundry so I can have clean, starched shirts and pressed pants for school. 'No boy of mine is gonna go around this town lookin like a hippie,' she'd tell me."

Now Artie drew himself up and looked at us defiantly.

"Last night . . . last night . . ." He was having trouble getting the words out. "Last night I said to her, 'I'm not dressing up for those honkies anymore. I'm gonna be my natural self, just dirty, black ole me.'"

He just stood there then with his fists clenched, like he was ready to take a swing at someone.

"What happened last night, Artie?" Mr. Innskeep asked softly. "Would you like to tell us?"

Artie looked surprised. His body relaxed and his voice got soft too.

"Last night my brother came back from New York looking for money to get another fix. He was feeling mean, so he told me that since I'm poking around asking so many questions for my honky report, I may as well know a few facts. That my ma ain't my ma. She's my grandmother. And my sister ain't my sister. She's my mother. 'You're putting me on, man,' I told him. And he said, 'Well, ask them yourself, black boy.'"

Artie's voice was so soft now that we could hardly hear him. We were all leaning forward, as if he was drawing us to him.

"Did you?" Mr. Innskeep asked in a louder voice, I suppose, hoping Artie would follow his lead.

"I couldn't ask my sister," Artie said, more loudly now. "She's off singing with some band. But I asked my ma, and she near fainted dead away. She broke down and cried and asked the Lord to forgive me, but then she admitted it was true. My sister, I mean my ma, she didn't want no part of me, because she wanted to be a singer, and my ma, I mean my grandma, she said one baby more or less wasn't gonna matter after all she'd raised. So she just tucked me in like I was her chick, and brought me here to Southhaven so I could grow up in some decent way. She says the others all went bad one way or other in New York. I'm her only hope. She says I'm gonna be a big man someday and make her life worthwhile."

"She may just be right too," said Mr. Innskeep. And then to break the tension, he smiled and added, "But no matter how big you get, keep on wearing jeans. They look good on you."

"I'm gonna wear them from now on," Artie replied with a grin, hitching them up as he spoke. "My ma, I mean my grandma, she, well, she promises she's not gonna try to control me so much anymore. She says she's gonna get her a good night's sleep from now on. And then she won't have to fall asleep in church no more."

This got a big laugh from the class, and he got a big applause too as he sat down.

I guess it was then I realized that this was the first time that no one laughed or snickered during a class. We were learning to be really nice and supportive to one another, as if we were all in the same family boat.

Mr. Innskeep was beaming now. "You see that no matter what the situation, the truth is always best," he told us. "Sometimes we think that a small lie is kinder, but in the long run it turns out to be more cruel, more destructive. It bores like a worm into family relationships until there is no trust left. It was very wise of Artie's grandmother to level with him when he confronted her with what he had heard."

"You're totally right," Stephanie called out. "I know it's not my turn, but I just want to say that I found out my grandmother isn't totally bonkers after all. When she realized I was interested in what she had to say—I mean totally—she started talking as sane as anyone about her life with my grandfather."

"We'll be *totally* waiting to hear about that on Monday," said Mr. Innskeep. "Now I think there's still time for Kevin Johnson, who'll be disappointed if he doesn't get his turn today."

"I won't be disappointed at all," said Kevin on his way up front. "I'm going to be totally boring. I didn't discover anything I didn't know before."

He seemed disappointed not to be able to shock us with some dramatic revelation—especially after all we'd been through with Hortense and Artie.

"My parents and their parents were all born in this area. No one went anywhere or did anything special. My grandfather went bankrupt in the Depression, but he paid all his debts back. My father was 4F during the war because of flat feet, but he hasn't missed a day of work in his life. He never has colds . . ." He went on and on like this in his usual singsong voice, and sat down quickly as soon as he was done.

"That was interesting, Kevin," said Mr. Innskeep encouragingly. "It's families like yours that are the backbone of this country. And I believe it was the Chinese philosopher Chuang Tzu who said, 'The best traveler stays at home.' "

With that the bell rang, as if on cue. We all grabbed our books and left.

"Have a good weekend," Mr. Innskeep called after us, like he always does on Fridays.

As I said, that class was a turning point for everyone. Maggie seemed totally shaken on the ride home.

"I'm a fraud," she said. "A total cop-out."

"What do you mean?"

"A coward! A zero! A fake!"

"Why?"

"I haven't been honest with myself, that's why. I've been telling you not to give up on your search, and giving advice to other kids about theirs. And all the time I've been saying I can't do anything because it will hurt Lisa."

"Well, won't it?"

"Maybe it will, maybe it won't. But that's not the real reason. The fact is that I've been afraid to look up my own grandparents and find out about my father."

"It's not too late, Maggie," I said, thinking of Sue's words to me.

"You're missing the point. I'm still afraid. Afraid of what I'll learn. It must be something terrible if Lisa won't tell me, and my own grandparents don't want to see me."

"What makes you think they don't want to?"

"Lisa said so. But anyway, they'd come around if they cared, wouldn't they? They don't live that far away."

"Maybe they've got a good reason."

"That's what I'm afraid of. And besides, I've got my pride. If they can do without me, I can do without them."

Suddenly Maggie's situation seemed very much like mine. It's terrible when people disappear on you and you don't know the reason. You think it might be your fault.

"I'll go with you to find them if you want me to," I told her.

"You will?" Her voice sort of broke here, as if it was the most amazing thing in the world that her best friend would help her. Maggie wasn't so self-confident after all.

"Of course I will. After all you've done for me, how could you doubt it?"

"I'd like you to come—for the ride," she said.

Then she pulled in to the Spice Box and we had hot fudge sundaes with extra nuts sprinkled on top.

twenty

When Maggie makes up her mind to do something, she does it right away—unlike me. I have to think about it, circle around it, suffer over it, and wait a long time before taking the first step.

We made plans for her to pick me up at ten the next day, which was a Saturday. I grabbed my coat when I heard her honk.

"Why doesn't she come in?" Mom asked, looking out through the window.

"We're in a hurry," I said, giving her a peck on the cheek.

"Where are you going in such a hurry on Saturday morning?"

"To the library. We have lots of work."

"I'm very impressed," said Mom. And she was.

"I slipped out without any hassle," Maggie told me when I got in the car. "Lisa was still sleeping. She had a long meeting last night. Her group is going to sit in at the new nuke plant in New Hampshire, and no one is going to move until they're carted away."

"Will they go to jail?"

"Probably. But they just get booked for overnight."

"Still, it's pretty brave."

"Yeah, I guess it is," said Maggie, as if realizing it for the first time. "Imagine getting arrested just because you want to save the world from blowing itself up."

We took the highway west from Southhaven, and in about

twenty minutes we reached the exit for Andersonville, where her grandparents lived.

"My name should really be Winston, like theirs," Maggie said. "But Lisa made me take Alan's. She said it was easier for us all to have the same name."

It was hard for me to think of her as Maggie Winston, rather than as the Maggie Brooks I knew. But then I could have been Lori Goldman. . . . And if I were, would I still be me?

Maggie's grandparents lived in an old section of the town. Their house sat on a narrow lane just off the main street.

"At least they don't need a car," Maggie commented. "They can just walk around the corner to the shops."

The house had obviously seen better days. Now it looked shabby and neglected; the paint was peeling around the windows and tall weeds were shooting up in the patches of dry grass that must have been a lawn once.

We let ourselves in at the gate and walked up the path to the rickety front steps. The house was what you call Victorian, with tall narrow windows and a round turret on top like the House of the Seven Gables.

Maggie stood there on the porch for a minute, and then picked up the knocker. It slammed with a thud against the door.

We listened, but we didn't hear any activity inside. "Maybe they're still asleep," I said. I had noticed that a lot of the shades were drawn.

"Old people get up early," she whispered. It was really weird. There she was making that noise with the knocker, and yet whispering to me as if she was afraid someone would hear.

She slammed the knocker down again.

This time we heard shuffling steps inside.

"Who's there?" asked a man's voice from the other side of the door.

For the first time I saw Maggie absolutely speechless. I realized we hadn't made any plans about what we were going to say once we got here.

"Do the Winstons still live here?" Maggie replied. Her voice came out with a quaver, as if she had something in her throat.

The man opened the door a crack, keeping it on the safety

chain. "What do you want?" he asked. He wasn't exactly unfriendly, just cautious. It was clear he wasn't used to having people come unannounced to his door.

"Are you Mr. Winston?" Maggie asked so timidly you'd have thought she was hoping he wasn't.

"I am," he said, closing the door and then opening it again with the chain off. He must have figured that two young girls who knew his name weren't going to give him any trouble.

"And who are you?" he asked. He seemed very friendly now, even though he still kept the door half closed.

"I'm Maggie—Maggie Brooks."

For a moment I thought the old man was going to keel over. He grasped the door and hung on as if it was the only thing holding him up.

"Mother," he cried, "come quickly!"

Then he let go of the door and grabbed Maggie. I mean really grabbed her, as if he wasn't going to let her get away. She slid into his arms as easily as a child, and the two of them just stood there sobbing.

Now Maggie's grandmother appeared at the door. She looked as startled as I was by the scene.

"What's the matter, Dad?" she asked nervously.

"Mother, it's the baby! Leonard's baby!"

"The baby!" she cried. She put out her arms and Maggie went to her. Now she was crying too, and then I burst out crying, and we were all bawling together on that porch, except that I had to hold on to the railing to comfort myself.

After a while Maggie's grandfather looked over at me. "This is your friend?"

"This is Lori," Maggie sobbed, wiping her eyes.

"Come on in, Lori," he said, very graciously. He was back in control of himself. "Come in, both of you."

We followed his tall, erect figure through the narrow corridor into a dark front room. "Let's talk in here," he said. "Mother, pull up the shades."

Maggie's grandmother was all smiles now. She was so tiny and wrinkled that I couldn't see any resemblance to Maggie. But Maggie definitely had her grandfather's green eyes and white skin.

The sunlight flooded into the room, and the old couple blinked as if they weren't used to such brilliance.

"She's the spitting image of him," Maggie's grandfather said. "It's Leonard's baby, all right."

"Can I get either of you some juice and cookies?" Maggie's grandmother asked.

"No, thank you," Maggie said. "I'm too excited to eat anything."

She turned to me.

"No, thank you."

"I'll get you some milk then," she insisted. "You must be thirsty."

"Sit down, Mother," said Mr. Winston. "We've waited a long time for this moment. We're not going to waste any more time getting things no one wants."

He reached over to a table behind the couch and picked up a photo album lying there. He wiped a thin layer of dust off it before opening it on the coffee table in front of us.

"This was your father when he was a boy," he said. "And here he is when he was your age. Sixteen."

"You know my age?" Maggie said.

"We sure do. We used to send you birthday presents, but your mother . . . well, she didn't think it was a good idea."

Tears started rolling down Maggie's cheeks again as she looked at the pictures of her father. He did look a lot like her —the same dark hair and wide mouth and the same chin jutting out just enough to be strong, but not too much. There were pictures of him in his uniform when he went off to war, his officer's cap over his forehead—in those, he stared out at us like a movie star. But there was no Hollywood ending to the story Maggie's grandfather told us.

He said that Maggie's father was never the same after coming back from Korea. He had a nervous breakdown shortly after Maggie's birth, and had to be hospitalized. He was in a military hospital for a year, and then, when he got out—it was hard for her grandfather to tell us—he took an overdose of drugs. He left a letter saying he didn't want to be a burden to anyone.

"It was the war," Maggie's grandmother said, shaking her

head over and over, as if she still couldn't believe it. "The war."

"He'd seen too much," her grandfather said. "His buddies killed before his eyes. He was too sensitive."

And then, glancing over at his wife, who was still shaking her head, he added, "Mother's never gotten over it. He was our only child. . . . But you probably know all this."

"No . . . my mother never told me," Maggie said.

"It was hard on her too," her grandfather replied. "A young widow with a baby. She started drinking too much. We were worried about her taking proper care of you. We petitioned the court for your custody." He stopped for a minute to catch his breath. "It was a bitter battle. And after that, she refused to let us visit you."

"She wouldn't let us see the baby," Maggie's grandmother kept repeating while he spoke.

"In some ways I understand," he said. "She was getting remarried. She wanted a new life. And maybe she was still afraid we'd try to steal you away."

Maggie was wide-eyed while he was talking. Then she went over to her grandmother and the two of them just held each other.

This brought another round of tears from everyone, including me. It was like a short rain squall, however, because Maggie's grandmother suddenly stood up and announced that she was bringing these young ladies something to drink no matter what anyone said.

She came back with a tray filled with three kinds of juices and some cookies and crackers. We started telling them about Buckeye High and our history assignment.

"Why didn't you come sooner?" Mr. Winston said.

"I was afraid you wouldn't want to see me," Maggie replied softly.

"Not want to see you? We've been living for this day!" he exclaimed.

"We knew you'd come," her grandmother said. "You're Leonard's daughter. You'd have to have his spirit."

"I'm going to visit you all the time from now on," Maggie promised when we got up to go. "You're my grandparents."

Her grandmother gave us a big bag of cookies to eat in the car, and everyone hugged everyone—including me. Her grandparents walked us to the gate, and stood there waving as we drove off.

twenty-one

I thought Maggie would just drop me off at my house, but she drove over to the Spice Box instead. We didn't even want the chocolate sundaes this time, but we ordered them anyway—it was part of our ritual.

"I guess my father's death had a lot to do with Lisa's drinking," Maggie said. We sat there quietly, thinking about this. "And maybe she's trying so hard to save the world because she wasn't able to save him."

"You mean you think she feels guilty?"

"Something like that."

We sat there just poking at the ice cream without much interest. I thought I'd burst if I even licked the spoon after all the cookies I'd devoured to please Maggie's grandmother.

"But it wasn't Lisa's fault," Maggie said. "It's what war does to people. It destroys their lives even when it doesn't kill them outright. It destroyed hers then."

"Still, she could have told you," I said.

"Maybe she thought it would hurt me to know," Maggie replied. "My grandparents didn't say it in so many words, but my father was crazy at the end."

"No," I protested.

"He was in a mental hospital."

"A military hospital."

"The military have hospitals for the insane too. Lisa probably didn't want me to brood about it. I understand."

I really admired Maggie for saying that. And it turned out to be true. Later, when she told Lisa that she had met her grandparents, Lisa wept and apologized for keeping them from her. She said she hadn't been able to bear for Maggie to know her father had committed suicide. And she'd never been able to face the reality of it herself. She had really loved him. She was angry at him for cracking up and at his parents for trying to take her baby away. She'd tried to escape everything by drinking, and then by denying the past. But now she understood that she'd only been hurting herself—and Maggie.

"You carry the past with you," she told Maggie, "in everything you do."

Maggie felt much better after their talk, and closer to Lisa now that this secret wasn't between them anymore. It was as if she understood her mother for the first time.

After that, Maggie really leveled with the class. I mean, she didn't hold anything back.

"I was afraid to look up my grandparents because I thought they might reject me," she said. "And there they were, waiting for me all that time. It proves that we have to confront things in life, even when it's difficult."

"That's totally right," Stephanie murmured, almost like an "amen."

And everyone began talking at once about how they were never going to run away from anything again. I sat there pretending to agree with them, but knowing that I was still running away. I was still hiding the truth about myself. Once you have a secret that you've told so many lies to protect, it's not easy to give it up.

So I just kept on with my research on orphanhood. Mr. Innskeep had lent me some books on the history of childhood, and I dug up a few in the school library on child welfare. It was unbelievable. In the nineteenth century, kids whose parents had died or disappeared were thrown into poorhouses with petty criminals and destitute people. Or they were "bound out," which means they were given as free labor to families that wanted them.

Homeless kids from New York were just pulled off the streets and sent west in "orphan trains" to any family that would take them. The myth was that they'd be getting a better life in "good Christian homes," but actually they were supposed to help on the farms and factories out there.

It really upset me to read about those poor kids. I even dreamt about being forced onto one of those orphan trains heading for nowhere. When the train made its stop at each little backwater, I got lined up with the others—we were like slaves on the auction block.

FARMER:	How 'bout that boy? Looks like he has strong muscles.
WIFE:	No, I'm hankerin' for a girl. She kin help me with the cleanin' and cookin'.
TRAIN CONDUCTOR:	Take 'em both. It don't cost you nothin'.
FARMER:	I'd druther have two boys.
WIFE:	Well, I'd druther have a girl. I want *that* one. *(Points to me)*
FARMER:	Nope. She's too scrawny. Not worth the food it'd take to fatten 'er up.
WIFE:	I don't need no fat girl. I kin manage this one fine. *(She puts her claw-like hands around my neck and starts to drag me off with her)*
ME:	Never! Never! I won't go with you! I won't! I won't!

I woke up that night with both Mom and Dad standing over me.

"You were calling out in your sleep, Cookie," Dad said. He had always called me Cookie when I was very young, but he hadn't done it for a long time.

I sat up and hugged him, and then I hugged Mom. I held on to them for a few minutes, and then I lay back and sobbed into the pillow.

"Was it a bad dream?" Mom said gently.

"Very bad."

"Well, nothing's going to get you, Cookie. Not while we're here," Dad said.

"It was only a dream," Mom said. "You're probably upset about Mike. Go back to sleep, dear."

twenty-two

Chris and I were doing it now. I mean all the way. It sort of happened after he gave me the ring. He said I should get birth control pills, but I was afraid our doctor would tell Mom. And I just couldn't go to a total stranger. So he always brought rubbers with him, and we'd park in our place. And it somehow seemed right, even though I knew I'd never marry him. Even if I got pregnant.

I could really sympathize with some of the girls in our class now—the ones who said they'd rather take a chance than use anything. At first I'd thought it was foolish, but now I understood that they didn't want it to seem like they were expecting something—which it would if they were all prepared. As I said earlier, some of them, like Molly Pendleton, did get pregnant and drop out of school, and most of them refused to give their babies up for adoption. That gave me something to think about. Why hadn't my mother kept me?

I knew I didn't want to get pregnant. The first month after Chris and I started doing it, I got really nervous a few days before my period, and then panicky when it was late. I'm irregular so it's hard for me to know what's going on. I'd keep thinking that maybe the rubber had a hole in it, or had slipped, and I was pregnant. I knew I couldn't get an abortion—after all, I might have been an abortion. But I also knew I didn't want to have a baby—not now. I wanted to go to college and maybe even drama school. If I got pregnant, I'd have to drop out of school and go to work to support the baby. It made me kind of understand what Barbara Goldman must have gone through when I thought about things that way. But still I knew I would never give my baby up for adoption like she did.

Barbara Goldman.

I might have waited years to find her if it hadn't been for Tony and Sue. All the time I was avoiding them, they were hard at work trying to help me.

One night Sue called and asked me to come over. When I started hedging that I had a lot of homework, she said she had a problem and needed me.

So I went. I thought maybe something had happened between her and Tony. But when I got there, Tony was sitting in the living room with her.

"What's the matter?" I asked. "Anything serious?"

"Oh, Lori, we were just lonely for you, that's all," Sue said. "We haven't seen you for so long."

But she had a funny smile on her face, like she was up to something.

"There isn't any problem?" I asked.

"Well, not exactly a problem," she said. "Would you call it a *problem*, Tony?" she asked turning to him.

"I'm not sure what the legal term for it is," he said slowly, as if giving it serious thought.

"Hey, what's going on?" I said. "You asked me to come over for something."

"Really, just to talk," Tony said. "You've been neglecting us."

"I've had rehearsals almost every day—and then there's Mike," I explained.

"How is he doing?" Sue asked, the smile gone now.

"He's doing okay, I guess. I haven't seen him. My folks go every Saturday."

"Tell them to give him our best," Sue said.

And then we all just sat there looking at each other. Sue was twiddling her thumbs and Tony's leg was jiggling up and down. I couldn't understand what their game was.

"Tony's been doing some interesting work lately," Sue said. "Why don't you tell her about it, Tony."

We both looked at Tony.

He got up and started pacing back and forth as he spoke. "Well, it's been interesting to *me*," he said. "We've been working on marriage law at school, which has meant looking up old documents to see how they were drawn up in the past and . . . and . . ."

He looked helplessly over at Sue.

"And he came across some really interesting marriage documents," Sue took over for him. I'd never seen her so involved with Tony's work before.

"He found George Washington's," I said, trying to be funny.

"Better than that," Tony said.

"Abraham Lincoln's."

"Your getting closer in time. But not close enough," he said.

"Theodore Roosevelt."

"Closer. But why do you assume a man?"

Now it *was* turning into a game. "Eleanor Roosevelt," I said, and from the look on his face I thought I'd guessed it.

"I've always admired Eleanor Roosevelt as a first lady," he said after a short pause. "And the woman I'm thinking of is second to no one."

"Come on, Tony, I give up," I said.

"Never give up, Lori," Tony replied, real serious now. "The name is—Barbara Goldman."

I felt my heart leap into my mouth—if that's possible. It leapt all over the place. It's a good thing I was sitting down. I felt like the breath had been knocked out of me. "What do you mean?" I managed to say at last.

"Just that. With Sue's help I managed to find Barbara Goldman's wedding certificate. It's not the same as finding her. But it's the next best thing."

Sue came over and sat down next to me on the couch. "It was Tony's idea," she said. "I just helped with the details." And then to Tony: "Tell her the background."

Tony pulled up a chair so that he was sitting directly opposite me, looking me full in the face.

"Those marriage contracts set me thinking," he said. "I knew your mother had to be attractive to have a daughter like you, so I figured she probably got married some time in the last sixteen years."

"And then he thought of looking for her wedding certificate," Sue said excitedly.

"But where? That was the question," Tony continued. "If I was lucky, it would be close by. So I decided to try New York, New Jersey, Pennsylvania, and even Connecticut. For all we knew she might be living a few blocks away."

"We sent checks to all four states with a request for Barbara Goldman's wedding certificate within a period of ten years after your birth," Sue picked up the story.

"It was a gamble, but it paid off," Tony added. "A copy of the certificate came in from New Jersey. It looks like she was married in her parents' home ten years after she had you."

"Oh, my God, I can't believe it!" I said.

"It's crazy," Tony went on. "You can get anyone's records on practically anything, but you can't get your own records if you're adopted."

He handed me the certificate. I could hardly hold it my hand was shaking so much. There was my mother's signature. It was proof that she existed. Large, bold letters, as if she was proud of what she was doing. She was twenty-nine then. Her husband's name was Bernard Botway.

"But that's not all," Sue said. "We found out where they are now."

"Sue really did it," Tony said. "I never would have had time."

"It wasn't all that difficult," Sue said. "I went into New York on my Thursday afternoon off and went through phone books at the public library. When I didn't see them listed in New Jersey, I tried New York—all the boroughs."

"And she found them—at a Riverdale address," Tony said proudly.

Now Sue handed me a slip of paper. "Here's the address and the phone number," she said. "Oh Lori, I told you we'd do it. And we did. All you've got to do now is decide how you want to contact her—by phone or by mail."

And when I didn't say anything, she added, "I'd call.

Remember at the Search and Find meeting everyone seemed to think that was better than writing."

"Maybe later," I said uncertainly.

"I wouldn't delay it too long—she might move," Sue said playfully. She was really on a high.

"I have to think about it for a while," I said firmly.

"Sure . . . sure I understand," she said, but she was clearly disappointed. I guess she thought I'd run to the phone right then and there.

"It's your ball game," Tony said, trying to ease the situation. "You give the signal, and we'll be there when you need us."

"Thanks," I said, tucking the certificate and the slip of paper into my jeans pocket and getting up to go. I felt like a real wet blanket but I couldn't help it. I just knew I couldn't act then. I had to wait.

Back in my room I put both pieces of paper into my address book, and the address book into my bottom desk drawer. Under a notebook. And I let them sit there. But sometimes late at night, I'd take them out and look at my mother's handwriting and at her address and phone number. I'd try to picture her again—a young woman with eyes like mine; a fat, frowsy woman in a faded housedress; a painted Eighth Avenue whore retired to the countryside after marrying a rich patron; a glamorous movie star with a large sun hat puttering in her Riverdale garden. I saw her house located on a river, with a broad green lawn sloping down to the bank. She would be sitting there alone, thinking of me. Wondering how I'd made out in life.

All I had to do was call that phone number and I would know who she was.

But I couldn't do it—yet.

twenty-three

It was a good thing our two-week spring vacation came then. I don't think I could have concentrated in school. It was like I had a nuclear bomb in my possession that might go off at any second. I felt elated, but I also felt as if I was going to die.

When Chris said good-bye to me before he left for California to visit his folks, who'd just returned from their round-the-world trip, I was both sorry to see him go, and relieved. I wanted to be alone. But I wondered if I'd be there when he came back. I mean the me that was me. Me, Lori Elkins, the girl he thought he loved, but hardly knew.

Maggie had talked Lisa and Alan into taking Jack with them to Key West, Florida—the new "in" place to be. Ernest Hemingway once lived there, and Tennessee Williams still did.

"I'll just faint if I see Tennessee Williams on the street," Maggie said before leaving.

"At least Jack will be there to pick you up," I quipped.

During spring vacation, our house was totally quiet. Mike was still at the treatment center, and now Mom and Dad were visiting him every Saturday. They'd leave early in the morning and not come back till evening. All week they seemed to be waiting for just that day.

I wanted to visit Mike, but I was afraid to go near that place. Ms. Barnes had said I needed a psychiatrist. What if I got there and Mike's doctor saw how messed up I was? They say psychiatrists can see right through you. Sometimes I'd wake up in the night in a cold sweat. It was like everything familiar was slipping away from me.

I told Mom and Dad that I had play rehearsals every weekend or else I'd go see Mike with them.

"I hope he's not hurt," Mom said. "I'll tell him about the play."

"What do you talk about?"

"Nothing complicated. I report on how Winkie keeps going to his room looking for him. And how his friends and teachers are calling to find out how he is."

"How is he—really?"

"He seems calmer," said Dad. "But he doesn't say much. He's going to the school they've got on the grounds."

"And he's doing well," Mom added.

"Will he be home soon?"

"I hope so," said Mom. But she didn't smile as she said it.

Everyone in my class was either on their research trips or off, like Maggie, with their families. Sue called almost every night when she came home from work. She'd brought a baby chimpanzee home to feed on the bottle and I went over a few evenings to help. But mostly I just lay around the house and listened to records and wrote lyrics. And slept. How I needed sleep.

At the end of the second week of vacation Sue, Tony, and I were sitting on Sue's porch with the chimpanzee. He was much fatter now and was snoozing in her arms just like a human baby.

"Honestly, I don't know how you can wait to call that number," Sue said for the umpteenth time. "I'd just burst if I waited this long."

"And then what would we do?" asked Tony, squeezing her.

Sue slipped away from him. "You've got to take the plunge, Lori. You can't go on torturing yourself like this. You'll go crazy."

That really got to me. Of course she didn't mean crazy crazy —but it could happen. I could just go berserk like Mike and have to be locked away. I had to act. Now.

"You know what I mean, Lori?" Sue added.

"You're right," I heard myself saying. "I'll call."

They both looked at me. Even the chimp looked at me.

"What did you say?" Tony asked.

"I said I was going to call."

"That's what I thought you said. I just wanted to make sure."

Sue threw the chimpanzee at Tony and hugged me.

"When?" she asked exuberantly.

"Tomorrow." It came out, just like that. I felt the way Maggie must have when she decided to go see her grandparents. She didn't hesitate from that moment. She was decisive.

"Really?"

"Cross my heart and hope to die."

Sue hugged me again. You would have thought it was her mother, she was so excited.

By now the chimp had gotten excited too, and was holding out its arms to her. She took him back and rocked him gently. He must miss his real mother, I thought. We had a lot in common, that chimp and I.

"You're sure you're ready?" Tony double-checked.

I shook my head yes.

The chimpanzee shook his, and Sue hugged him too.

The next day was Saturday, which meant Mom and Dad would be off seeing Mike. Chris would be back on Sunday, and Monday was school again. If I was going to do it, tomorrow was my last chance.

Tony is going to be a really good lawyer someday. He always thinks of all the angles.

"Plan what you're going to say before you call," he suggested now. "Think through the possible responses she might have. Be prepared for anything."

"That's right," Sue agreed. "Remember that guy at the Search and Find meeting who thought he'd found his mother."

It will be different for me, I wanted to say. My mother would never deny who she was. She had to be someone special. After all, she was *my* mother.

All that night I went over the possible scenarios in my head. It was like writing a play. Only now I wasn't Emily Webb or Lori Elkins—I was Baby Goldman.

I imagined it happening something like this:

ME: Hello, is this the former Barbara Goldman?
BARBARA: Yes. Who's calling?
ME: I was born on May twenty-third, sixteen years
             ago. Does that mean anything to you?
BARBARA: My baby! I've been waiting for this call.
ME: Then you are my mother?
BARBARA: I am.
ME: I just want to know why you gave me up.
BARBARA: I had to. He wouldn't marry me. But I've been
             sorry ever since. I've never stopped thinking of
             you.
ME: I just want to learn about my roots.
BARBARA: Can we meet this instant? Anywhere. You
             name the place and I'll be there.
ME: I could come to your home.
BARBARA: Come immediately. I'll be watching in the
             window.

I didn't get any sleep that night. Even though one part of me believed that my mother would be glad to hear from me, another part feared she would hang up the phone. That she would be angry I was interrupting her life. That she would hate me for coming back.

Mom and Dad were already off to see Mike when I came downstairs that morning. Mom had left the refrigerator stocked with things for me in her usual efficient way. There was so much food you'd think I did nothing all day but eat, or that they were going to be away for weeks.

I had set the alarm for ten so I wouldn't oversleep. It would be just like me to sleep through the whole day. Dad used to joke that I could sleep through a UFO's landing on our front lawn. And I guess I could, if it came too early.

I dressed carefully that day—my best French jeans and a T-shirt with LOVE across it. I even put on some lipstick and eyeliner—as if she'd be able to see me through the phone. I wanted to look good so I would sound good. So my mother would think her daughter was a knockout and want to meet her.

I took the slip of paper with the number on it out of my address book and put it on the desk by the phone. I could hardly breathe. I forced myself to pick up the receiver. But I kept dialing the wrong numbers and I had to keep hanging up and starting over again. Finally I just gave up and sat there for about five minutes hoping I could calm down a little.

I almost jumped out of my skin when the phone rang—it was as if it had a life of its own. I grabbed it. For one wild moment I thought it could be *her* calling me. I had read stories of strange instances of telepathy, where two people far away from each other are thinking the same thing at the same time.

"Lori, it's Mom," came over the wire.

My heart sank. "I know."

"Honey, I hope I didn't wake you. I forgot to take Winkie's hamburger out of the freezer. Could you do that for me? Otherwise he'll have nothing to eat."

"I'll take care of it, Mom."

"Thank you, dear. I'm forgetting everything. I guess these trips back and forth are getting to me. Did you have breakfast?"

"I'm fine, Mom. Give Mike my love."

"I will. I have to go now. The doctor is going to speak to us any minute."

What would she say if she knew what I was doing? I felt like a real traitor as I hung up the phone and went downstairs to the kitchen. Winkie was sitting outside in the back, waiting for me. Mom must have really been cracking up—by her standards. She'd forgotten to mention that detail—to let him in. I opened the door and picked him up and hugged him, even though his paws were filthy and his breath smelled of the garbage he had gotten into. For a spoiled dog who turned his nose up at canned dog food, he sure was a scavenger.

"Winkie," I said, "you've got to sit with me while I make my call. I need you to give me courage."

I put him down, and he followed me upstairs and sat loyally at my side.

"Wish me luck," I said.

But he had already lost interest. He slid down to a reclining position and had the nerve to close his eyes, as if what I was about to do was the most boring instead of the most important thing in the world.

This time I dialed very carefully.

A child answered the phone. "Hullo."

I hadn't expected that. I almost hung up, but I forced myself to say, "Is Mrs. Botway there?"

"Who is it?" the child demanded.

"A friend. Is she there?"

"What's your name?"

"What's *your* name?" I countered.

"Muffy."

She was clearly at the age when you love to talk on the phone—to anybody. I went through that myself. Luckily the receiver was taken out of her hands just then.

"Hello," a woman's voice said. It sounded nice.

"Hello. Is this Mrs. Botway?"

"Yes."

"Were you Barbara Goldman?"

"Yes. Who is this?"

For a moment I forgot who I was. It was like forgetting your line in a play. Then I recovered. "My name is Lori Elkins. I was born on May twenty-third, sixteen years ago. Does that mean anything to you?"

There was a silence, and a gasp: "My God!" Then she recovered herself and asked cautiously, "How did you get this number?"

"A friend found it," I said meekly.

"What did you say your name is?"

"Lori Elkins. I was adopted through the Rocking Cradle. I think you're my mother."

"Can I call you back?"

"Yes."

I gave her the number. And she said she'd call right back.

I began shaking after I hung up the phone. I couldn't believe I had done it. She hadn't exactly said she was my mother, but then she hadn't said she wasn't either. She probably couldn't talk with the child there. But would she call back?

I almost fainted when the phone rang three minutes later, it startled me so. But it was only one of Mom's friends from the PTA. I couldn't get her off the line.

"Lori, don't forget to tell your mother that we're going to elect new officers next month and she should be thinking who would make a good treasurer. It's a hard job, you know. Sadie Thompkins just couldn't keep on with it, what with her twins reaching toddler age. It wears you out running after them—and two of them at that."

Finally I broke in that I heard someone at the door and had to get off. I put the receiver down real hard.

Still, I was relieved it hadn't been her. It gave me more time to pull myself together. I took Winkie by the front paws and danced around the room with him. He thought I was cracking up, and struggled to get free.

"Keep dancing, Winkie," I told him. "Imagine you are going to meet your real mother. Do you remember her? She must have had long golden ears like you. And long silky hair, and big black eyes."

I held his face next to mine and he licked my nose.

"No, I'm not your mother, idiot," I said, pushing him away. Then I found his brush and started grooming him as if he really was going to see his mother.

I kept brushing him and brushing him, but still the phone didn't ring. Maybe she'd tried to call me when I was on the phone with Mom's friend. And had given up. But would she give up so quickly? Wouldn't she try again?

I picked up a magazine and tried to read. But the pages were all a blur. I couldn't read stories about other people now, because there was only one story I was interested in—mine.

I paced my room for a while and then I opened my door and paced the upstairs hall. Winkie followed me back and forth for a few minutes, and then flopped down on the top step to watch me. He lay there, stretched out, his head on his paws, probably wondering what was happening to his safe little world. Mike gone, Mom forgetful, Dad worried, me crazy.

I sat down on the step with him and tried to see the world

from his point of view. Once he'd left his mother as a puppy, he never saw her again. We were his adopted family, and he seemed content with us. But when he whimpered in his dreams at night, gave short little yelps that didn't sound like him at all, was he longing for his lost mother? Or is it only humans who do that?

"Be glad you're not human," I whispered into his ear, which was unusually soft now that I had gotten rid of the tangles. He flapped his ears vigorously, as if shaking out my words.

From where I sat I could hear the ticking of the old grandfather clock downstairs. It had been in Mom's family for generations. Why was it called a grandfather clock? Did even time need a relationship to the past?

What was she doing—this woman who was probably my mother? Was she sitting on a step now with her dog? Or with the little girl who had answered the phone? Her life had gone on without me. Was she wondering what to do? Hoping I would just go away?

After a few hours had passed, I knew she wasn't going to call. Now I threw myself on my bed and lay there as if dead. I had heard her voice once. I would settle for that. It was obviously too late for us now. I should have understood that from the beginning. I was even kind of relieved.

And then the ring of the phone pierced the air. I leapt up and just listened to it ring—once, twice, three times. Then I grabbed the receiver.

"Hello!"

"Is this Lori Elkins?"

"Yes."

"Lori, it's me, Barbara Botway."

"I know."

"I'm sorry I couldn't call back sooner. I had to wait until everyone was out of the house."

I didn't know what to say.

"I never thought I'd ever hear from you," she went on. "It's a miracle." A pause. "How are you?"

And then we both laughed because it was so absurd, her asking me how I was.

"I'm fine, how are you?"

We laughed again. Only I guess they weren't real full laughs. We were too nervous.

"Do your parents know you're calling me?"

"No."

"I hope they won't mind."

"They'll be all right."

A pause.

"Can I meet you?" I blurted out. I hadn't planned to say it so soon.

There was another pause.

Then she said, "I'll have to figure out where. It can't be here. Not yet."

She was kind of mumbling to herself. Then she remembered me. "When is good for you?"

Strange—I hadn't even thought about when I could meet her, or how. School started again on Monday.

"You have school, don't you?" she said, as if reading my mind.

"Yes. But I'm free on weekends."

"Let's see, your area code was Connecticut." Now she sounded in control of things. "Do you live near New York? Or should I meet you somewhere halfway?"

"I come in to Manhattan all the time," I said, wanting to sound very grown up. "I could come in on Saturday."

"I'll try to clear my schedule, then. I'll just have to. Let's think of somewhere central. Do you have any ideas?"

I didn't.

"How about Rumpelmayer's? Do you know where it is?"

"Yes." (Mom and Dad used to take Mike and me there for ice cream after we went sight-seeing in the city.)

"I think that's as good a place as any. If it's not too crowded. Great desserts. How about one o'clock? We can have lunch."

"Yes."

"Remember, it's on Central Park South near Sixth Avenue. One o'clock. This Saturday."

"Yes." She must have thought I was a half-wit, the way I couldn't say anything but "Yes."

"I'll wear a bright scarf around my neck . . . so you'll recognize me."

She gave that nervous laugh again. And then, "Good-bye, Lori."

"Good-bye."

I put the receiver down softly so as not to disconnect the magic of that call. Then I hugged Winkie and ran over to Sue's.

"Oh, Lori, I can't believe it," Sue kept saying. And she made me repeat every word of the conversation, over and over.

"She sounds wonderful," Sue cried. Taking my hands she twirled me around the room.

And then we both burst into tears.

The chimpanzee was sitting in the playpen Sue had borrowed from a friend. It looked up at us as if it thought *we* were the ones who should be heading for a zoo.

twenty-four

       Mr. Innskeep's class was absolute bedlam that Monday.

Everyone was full of all they'd accomplished over vacation. I stayed quiet, glad that no one asked me anything. After all when your parents are orphans, like mine were supposed to be there's nothing to get excited about. And I wasn't about to pretend any enthusiasm over the history of child welfare.

Maggie hadn't come back yet. I was dying to tell her about calling my mother. I had to share it with someone. I decided the moment had come to level with Chris.

"Let's go to the Fiery Ox after school," he called to me in the hall. "I've got a lot to tell you."

"And I've got a lot to tell you," I said. But there wasn't time for any more than that.

The Fiery Ox was almost empty—it doesn't really jump during the day. Chris and I had our choice of booths, and as soon as we'd ordered our hamburgers, I tried to think of how to tell him about my historic call. The trouble was that first had to confess that I was adopted.

I was so self-absorbed that it didn't occur to me to ask Chris how his vacation had been or what he had to tell me. I guess didn't really care. I just wanted to talk about myself.

I felt like a heroine in a play—a tragedy.

"Chris, I've been keeping something from you."

"What?" He looked startled—even worried.

"I don't know how to break it to you."

"What?" He was clearly alarmed.

"I'm adopted." I looked him straight in the eye, but instead of finding amazement, I found relief.

"Is that all?"

"Is that *all*? Isn't that *enough*?" My voice got shrill on "enough."

"I mean I thought it was something really important, Lor. Like—you know."

I couldn't believe what he was hinting at. "You don't think being adopted is important?" I demanded.

"But I already knew that."

"You knew it?" I could hardly breathe.

"Sure, my aunt told me when I started going with you."

"How did she know? She doesn't know my parents that well."

"Someone must have told her. What's the big deal?"

"The big deal is that I'm going to secretly meet my *real* mother on Saturday." I thought that last should impress him.

But he didn't even bat an eye. "You shouldn't do that, Lor."

"Shouldn't do it?" I was speechless. "Why not?"

"It would hurt your folks."

"That's all you can say? That it would hurt my *folks*?"

"Well, I've gotten to like them. They're really good people. They raised you and love you."

"What about me?" I said. I could feel my throat tightening and my eyes brimming with tears. I was afraid I was going to start bawling right there in the Fiery Ox.

He must have been afraid I was too. He moved over to my side of the booth and put his arm around my shoulders. I pushed it off.

"You'll hurt yourself too," he said softly. "It doesn't matter who your real parents are. I love you just the way you are."

He tried to put his arm around me again, but I moved as far away as I could on the seat.

"Let's not talk about it anymore," he said. "It's not worth it."

"Let's not talk at all, Christopher Barlow," I said, jumping up and scrambling out of the booth. "You're an insensitive . . boor. I never want to talk to you again!"

And I ran out into the street and jumped on the first bus I saw going in my direction. I couldn't get over it. He'd known all along! And hadn't said anything. Did everyone at school know? I felt like a fool. Everyone knowing things about me that I didn't know they knew.

Why do the people who say they love you never want to talk about the things that matter most to you—the inner you, I mean? I felt like two people again. The outer me who went to school and dated Chris and acted like everyone else. And the inner me who was all alone, and didn't have any connection with anyone.

I didn't answer my phone when it kept ringing that night because I knew it was probably Chris. And I made a point of trying to avoid him in the halls the next few days. At first he'd grab my arm and say he had to talk to me, but I'd just pull away. Finally he took the hint. I guess he had his pride too. We started passing each other in school like strangers.

"What's going on with you and Chris?" Maggie asked when she came back later that week.

"Nothing's going on."

"That's what I mean."

"I decided to cool it for a while," I said mysteriously.

"Did you have a fight?"

"Nothing worth talking about."

She was in great spirits. Her face was bright pink (especially her nose, which was still peeling), and she had lost some weight.

"Jack got on great with Alan," she said.

"Not with Lisa?"

"Oh, she likes him all right. But she thinks he should be more concerned with preventing nuclear war than with preventing cavities. She says that nuclear fallout will make our teeth fall out faster than not flossing."

"And what does Jack say?"

"He says he'll love me even without teeth." She held out her leg to show me the gold ankle chain he'd bought her.

She was so full of Jack, I could hardly get a word in edgewise. Finally I had to stop her in mid-sentence: "Shut up, Maggie. I made the phone call."

She stood there with her mouth open. "You what?"

"I called my mother."

"That's what I thought you said. What happened?"

"I'm going to see her this Saturday."

"Oh, Lori!" She threw her arms around me and held me close. Then, changing her voice to Mrs. Webb's, she said, "My little girl Emily is going off to see her other mother. I do declare I'm jealous."

"I'll come back to you, Ma," I said, in Emily's voice.

"I just know you'll hit it right off," she wailed. "You'll forget about me. And after I raised you and everything."

"I'll still be your little girl, Ma."

"You'll like her better than me," Mrs. Webb howled. And then Maggie stopped and said in her own voice, "Wow, is that what your real mom is going to think?"

"Which one?"

"The adopted one, idiot. Have you told her?"

"Of course not. I'm not *that* much of an idiot."

"Are you going to?"

"Later. After I see what happens."

"Are you scared?"

"Totally." A little smile with that.

"Want me to go with you?"

For a moment I was tempted. I remembered walking with Maggie up the steps to her grandparents' house, and how glad they were to see us. But this was different. This was my mother. She might be embarrassed if someone else were there.

"I can do it, Maggie. I'm growing up."

"What are you going to wear?"

I hadn't even thought about that. What does one wear to meet the mother one has never known. Has such an outfit ever been designed?

"I'll just go in a diaper," I said.

"You'll catch cold. Want to borrow something?"

"Like what?"

"The long red dress I stole from Lisa."

We dissolved into gales of laughter at the thought of me going in to New York in that red chiffon chemise that looked like a nightgown.

"I think I'll settle for my madras skirt and vest. Or should I wear slacks?"

"She'll love you in anything."

"Will she, Maggie?"

"She'd better, or she'll have to deal with me."

twenty-five

I thought Mom and Dad would never get out of the house that Saturday morning. They were much more relaxed than I'd seen them since Mike had been gone. He'd actually been civil to them their last few visits. He'd told them all about working in the greenhouse and how his schoolwork was going. He even seemed concerned about not falling behind at his own school. For Mike, that was real progress.

"He was asking about you again, Lori," Mom said. "You really should come with us one of these trips. Even the doctor said so."

"The doctor?" That scared me. "What does he have to do with it?"

"He was wondering how you were feeling about all this."

"It's none of his business," I snapped, surprised at my own outburst. "I mean, Mike's his patient, not me."

"They like to see all the family members," Mom said.

I pictured the doctor sitting smugly behind his desk like Ms. Barnes. He wasn't going to get his hands on me.

"I told you I'll visit Mike *after* the play, Mom," I said firmly. "I'll have more time then."

"Do you honestly expect your brother to understand that his sister can't make time to visit him?"

"He will. Tell him I have to slay a dragon first."

"You what?"

"He'll know what I mean."

"Don't count on it," said my father, getting into his coat. They were really going, at last.

157

"What are your plans today?" Mom asked as they were on their way out.

"I'm going to rehearsal with Maggie. And then we're going back to her house to go over lines."

"Well, have a good time. And don't worry if we get home late tonight. We may play cards on our way back."

"Win a few dollars for me," I said. And then I added before Dad could open his mouth, "I know, don't count on it."

"This time you can count on it," said my father, with a big grin. "We're on a real winning streak, your mother and I."

As soon as they left, I ran over to Sue's, and she drove me to the train station.

"I could still go with you, Lori," she said for the umpteenth time. "I saved the day, just in case."

And for the umpteenth time I thanked her, and said I had to go alone.

She stood with me on the platform until the train came. As I boarded, and she started waving, I felt as if I was going off to the wars. In a way, I was, because I was going somewhere very far away—to that lonely place inside me—and I had the fear a soldier must have of what would happen there, and if I'd come back changed in some terrible way.

How can I explain it?

Going to meet your mother is a wonderful thing, but it's also terrifying. I kept thinking that seeing my mother's face for the first time would be like looking into the face of God. Like you know that God is out there, somewhere, but you're not allowed to see Him. When I was little there was a photograph of an old man on my aunt's piano in Chicago, and somehow I got the idea it was God's picture. I stared at it for a long time, because I really wanted to know what He looked like.

My mother's face was just as mysterious to me. No one had ever shown me a picture of her. It was so forbidden to see her that it frightened me that I was about to. It might be like gazing into a light that was too bright. Or like looking at an eclipse without dark glasses or a special filter. I've heard you can go blind if you do that—looking at what you're not meant to with the naked eye.

I walked up to Central Park South from the train station. For the first time I wasn't looking at people on the street, wondering if they were my parents. I was going to meet the woman who gave birth to me. I wondered if it showed on my face. If I had some special glow that ordinary people who grow up with their mothers don't have.

I got to Rumpelmayer's first. I knew I would. I was fifteen minutes early. What if she came an hour late? Or didn't come at all?

The last time I had been to Rumpelmayer's I was nine and Mike was six. We had driven in as a family to visit the United Nations, and had come here afterwards for a special ice cream treat. I could remember the excitement of it, and spotting the stuffed animals on the racks just inside the door. I had wanted a big lion, but Mom said everything was too expensive. She told me under her breath that it was ridiculous to pay those high prices when you could get toys like that much cheaper in a department store. But Mike grabbed a tiny giraffe and made such a scene when the folks said no that they finally gave in and bought it just to get him out of there. Mom said I could have something small too, but I was too proud to take her offer. We'd never gone there since.

I watched now as children spun through the revolving door into the Rumpelmayer wonderland. And it wasn't only this pastry shop that exuded a sense of fantasy—it was all of Central Park South with its posh hotels and elegant restaurants. The well-dressed people dashing by had much the dither of the White Rabbit: "Oh dear! Oh dear! I shall be too late!" One might even expect to see the Queen of Hearts riding off in one of the horse-drawn carriages that were lined up across the street, waiting to give tourists rides through the park.

I was Alice about to go through the looking glass into which I'd been peering all these years.

One o'clock. My mother was late.

One-fifteen. My mother was still late.

One-thirty. My mother was too late. What if she'd changed her mind and wasn't coming?

Then I saw her. I knew it was her even from a distance. She

was about my height and kind of slim, like me, with the same light brown hair, only hers was short. She was wearing a gray suit and a bright red scarf at her throat. She was walking quickly, looking straight ahead at the doorway, as if she expected someone to be there.

For a moment I panicked. What do you do when you meet your mother for the first time? Do you shake hands? Do you kiss her?

When she got up closer, our eyes met. She rushed towards me. "You must be Lori," she said. She put out both her hands and gripped mine firmly. "I'm sorry I'm late. The traffic was unbelievable."

"That's all right," I lied.

"Your hands are cold," she said. "Mine are always cold too."

Her eyes were gray, not brown like mine. That's the first thing I thought when I looked at her. She had my nose, but her face wasn't as round as mine. She was familiar and unfamiliar at the same time.

I liked her. The warmth of her greeting. Her energy. She put her hand on my shoulder as if we'd known each other forever, and together we spun through the revolving door. My legs felt like rubber, but somehow I managed to step out of it and to walk straight ahead—through the front room with the ice cream counter and the racks of stuffed animals, into the dining area just beyond.

A woman carrying menus began escorting us to a center table, but Barbara asked for one in back where it was quiet. I was glad the waitress came over right away, because it meant we had to look at the menu and could talk about things like whether we wanted a full luncheon or a la carte. I was too nervous to eat, but I ordered a shrimp salad because Barbara did. It seemed more grown up than a hamburger, though I asked for a Coke instead of tea, which Barbara was having.

"You can look at the dessert table later," Barbara said. "It has lots of wonderful cakes and fruit tarts."

I called her Barbara right from the start. I just couldn't call her Mother—she didn't seem like my mother—and I couldn't call her Mom, because I already had a Mom. Calling her

Barbara made her sound like a friend, which she was, in a way. I guess there just isn't a name for a relationship like ours.

When the waitress was gone, we looked at each other sort of shyly.

"You look a lot like I did at your age," Barbara said. "You have the same high forehead. It runs in the family." Our eyes met again, as if we were each searching for something. "But you're prettier than I was," she added.

We sat there just looking at each other.

I had planned to ask her so many things, but I couldn't think of a thing to say. You can't make small talk with a mother you've never seen before—and you can't just blurt out the big questions, like "Why did you give me away?" So I just sat there looking at her and feeling both alarmed and peaceful inside. It seemed natural to be with her, but also unreal. It was outside of time. In some never-never land. I was now the child who had never grown up, returned to that moment when we had gone separate ways.

Maybe because meeting each other was forbidden, there was a sense of danger—the unspoken knowledge that anything we said had the power to hurt as well as heal. It wasn't just the past that hung in the balance, but the future too.

"I never thought I'd see you again," she said, speaking first. "I still can't believe it." Tears filled her eyes and she took out a handkerchief. "I told myself I wasn't going to cry, and here I am already doing it."

I wiped a few tears that started trickling down my cheek with the back of my hand.

"Do your parents know you're here?" she asked. She seemed very concerned about my parents.

"No."

"I hope they won't mind. I don't think we're supposed to get together like this."

We smiled at each other like conspirators. That's what we were, in a way. It gave us a bond that seemed to dissolve the tension that had prevented our speaking before.

"How did you ever find me?"

I told her about the history assignment and how some friends had helped me search for her.

"That was very resourceful of you," she said. "I've seen some articles in the paper about adopted people searching, but I never thought you might be among them. Yet I wasn't really surprised when you called. I guess something in me always knew you would."

Again we just stared at each other.

"Driving here in the car, I tried to think of all the things I wanted to tell you, but I was worrying too much about how I looked. I've hardly slept since you called. I didn't want you to be disappointed."

"I was worried too," I said.

"I didn't know what to wear. Whether you wanted me to be elegant in a black dress with high heels, or casual in a pants suit with boots."

We both laughed.

"I like you the way you are," I said.

But instead of that making her happy, it made tears well up in her eyes again. She smiled deliberately, trying to blink them away.

"I'm not going to weep, I promise you," she said. "This is a happy occasion, and we're going to keep it that way."

Still, she took out her handkerchief again and dabbed at her eyes. I gave mine a swipe with my napkin.

"I've learned self-control over the years," she said. "I had to, or I wouldn't have made it."

We watched as the waitress filled our water glasses. Even this seemed to have a special importance.

"I haven't talked about anything to do with you for sixteen years," she went on when the waitress was gone. "I put it away somewhere. I had to forget. It was too painful. Everyone said it would be easy to go on with my life as if nothing had happened. I thought there was something wrong with me when I kept dwelling on it." She interrupted herself. "But I don't want to bother you with this."

"It's not bothering me," I said, trying to reassure her. "I want to hear everything."

"Of course you do," she said, looking directly at me again. "One of the things that really worried me was that you wouldn't understand why I had to give you up. I asked the social worker to put in the agency file that you came from a respectable family. You do. We have lots of professional people—lawyers, doctors, teachers. Though we have our black sheep too."

She laughed when she said that. She definitely had a sense of humor, and it helped.

"Let's see now, where should I begin?"

"From the beginning, I guess."

"Oh, Lori, where does anything begin? All right. I was nineteen by the time I had you. After I finished my first year of college, I got a job at a resort hotel in the Catskills to make some pin money, as we called it then. There were a lot of students there for the same reason. We had, you know, summer romances."

She had a habit of biting her lower lip, which I do too. (Could there be a gene for lip-biting?) Anyway, there we sat biting our lips as the waitress placed our shrimp salads in front of us.

"I didn't suspect I might be pregnant until I'd gone back to school," Barbara continued when we were alone again. "I couldn't believe it could happen to me. By the time I went to the doctor, I was already in my fifth month. I thought I'd faint when he told me."

She reached over and touched my hand. "Oh, Lori, I don't mean it the way it sounds. It has nothing to do with you."

"I understand," I said. And I did. I remembered how nervous I'd been about getting my period last month.

"He . . . my friend . . . your father . . . was a student at the University of California. I dropped him a note. I wasn't asking for anything, but I felt he should know. We'd had a lot of good times together, but neither of us thought it was love. Well, I guess maybe I thought it could be at the time. I decided that if he insisted on marrying me, I would."

She paused for a moment and gave her salad a half-hearted poke with her fork.

"Did he?" I asked.

"He never answered the letter. I never saw or heard from him again."

"I'm sorry," I said.

"Oh, Lori, I've never stopped being sorry. I've often wondered what might have been if he had answered it. When I told my parents, my father wanted to sue his family. But I wouldn't give him the name."

Neither of us was eating the salad. I mean it wasn't the kind of conversation that exactly made you hungry. Barbara kept poking at hers, but I didn't even do that.

"My mother was more understanding, but worried about what the neighbors would think. We lived in a small town in New Jersey. She arranged for me to go to a maternity home in New York. I stayed there until I surrendered you."

She took the handkerchief out of her purse again. " 'Surrendered' is the right word for it. The social worker told me that the best thing to do was to *surrender* you for adoption. I wanted you to have a good home with a family. I didn't think I could give you very much then."

She choked a little on this and drank some water. I took a sip too. I just couldn't look at her then.

"But when you were born and the nurse let me hold you, I changed my mind. You were so miraculous. Your little fingers clutched mine as if you liked me and didn't want to let me go. You had a little button nose and big dark eyes that seemed to have a lot of thoughts behind them. The nurse said you looked like an old soul."

"What's an old soul?" I asked.

"Someone who has been born more than once and therefore looks very wise. It made me think that maybe there was some special reason you had been born to me and that it would be wrong not to keep you. I tried to think of ways to support you —jobs I would get. But my mother got very angry when I spoke like that. She said it would ruin my life, and yours. That really got to me. I felt so guilty already about causing her and my father so much trouble. And I didn't want to ruin your life. Do you understand, Lori?"

I nodded. I understood only too well, but it still hurt to hear that my grandmother hadn't wanted me.

Barbara gave a weak smile. "You *are* a wise old soul. Wiser than me. I let the social worker convince me that other people could raise you better than I could just because they were married."

Now she popped a shrimp into her mouth and began chewing it in silence. I took one of mine but had a hard time swallowing it. It was strange to hear her referring to Mom and Dad this way.

"You were such a special baby, Lori. And I felt so worthless then. I thought it was the one good thing I could do—give you a chance in life. And so I signed the surrender paper, and left the hospital without you."

"Is the salad all right?" the waitress asked. I guess she had noticed that we weren't eating.

"Just fine," Barbara mumbled without looking up.

"And what did you do then?" I asked.

"I couldn't go back to school again, even though Mom wanted me to. And I didn't want to go home. For many reasons. My father hadn't come to the hospital. He didn't even ask if the baby was a boy or a girl. He didn't mean to be cruel, but he just wouldn't talk about it."

I could imagine my dad not wanting to talk about it either.

"So I took a room in Greenwich Village and got a job in a department store to put myself through night school. But for a long time I was so depressed I could hardly study. I'd wander through the children's section at the store touching the baby clothes. 'This would look adorable on her,' I'd think. I'd picture you in so many things."

She was having a hard time speaking now. Our eyes started getting teary again. I tried to picture that little baby too, but it was hard to connect it with me. We each reached into our purses at the same time, which made us giggle through our tears. I was determined not to cry. Not here in Rumpelmayer's. It would be too embarrassing.

"After college I got a job in advertising and forced myself to forget you. I had decided never to get married or have children. I'd be one of those tight-lipped old spinsters who kept her innermost thoughts from the world."

"But you did get married," I interrupted. "I saw the wedding certificate."

"Not until much later. He was an older man who worked in

my advertising agency. He'd been a bachelor all his life and didn't want children either. We are very close, but I've never told him about you."

"Who was the child who answered the phone?"

She smiled. "Women are very inconsistent creatures, Lori. As an old soul you must know that. I had no sooner gotten married than I wanted a baby. One that I could keep. I couldn't believe my luck when it was a girl. It was like a second chance."

"Does she look like me?"

"More like her father. Her name is Martha, but we call her Muffy. Would you like to see her picture?"

Now, this is weird. I didn't want to see my own sister's picture. Not then. I wanted to be the only child we were talking about that afternoon. I was actually jealous that Muffy was taking Barbara's attention away from me.

Barbara took a photograph wallet out of her purse and opened it to the first snapshot. I saw a little girl about four, with long blond hair and a red pinafore. She was clutching a doll that was dressed in a matching outfit.

"Actually, she's the spitting image of her father."

As she said it, I wondered if she thought I looked at all like *my* father. But I didn't want to ask anything then for fear it might hurt her feelings.

"She's cute," I said, handing the picture back to Barbara.

She gave me a curious smile, as if wondering what I was thinking. "Let's give up on the salads and try the dessert table now," she said, pushing her chair back and getting up. "People from all over the world bring their children to Rumpelmayer's for just this moment. And you deserve something sweet."

I still wasn't hungry, but I didn't want to hurt her feelings. I chose a piece of dark chocolate cake and she chose a raspberry tart. I felt very grown up back at the table when she asked me if I wanted coffee.

But neither of us could touch a bite. We just kept looking at each other. She said my folks had done a better job than she could have done. But she didn't ask anything about them. I told her about school and Maggie and the play. She had acted in plays in high school too and even tried writing a novel after she had me.

"It wasn't much good," she confessed. "Everything was too bottled up inside me then. In writing you have to expose yourself. I wasn't able to do that."

I knew exactly what she meant. Most of the time I wrote fantasies about far-off places I didn't know anything about.

"So I just stuck to the slick prose of advertising copy," she continued. "It was the easy way out. I didn't have to feel too deeply."

When the waitress came by with the check, she seemed surprised that we hadn't eaten our desserts. "I don't want to hurry you two," she said, "but I go off my shift now."

I watched Barbara pay with a credit card, and then I followed her out towards the exit.

"Have a good day," the waitress called after us.

"It's the best day of my life," Barbara replied, taking my arm. She stopped when we got to the toy animal rack near the soda fountain.

"I always wanted to buy you a stuffed animal," she said almost shyly, as if she knew it was too babyish now, but couldn't control the impulse. "It would make me very happy if you chose something, Lori."

I looked over the rack very self-consciously, trying to keep my dignity. But I have to admit there was an adorable brown buffalo and a furry white bear that I couldn't decide between.

"Which one do you like?" I asked her.

"Take the bear," she said. "I'm partial to bears."

When he was wrapped, the bear made a bulky package. I wondered how I was going to explain him to my folks.

It was Barbara who suggested the buggy ride. She must have felt as reluctant to part as I did. We were both giggling as we climbed into the open hansom and let the driver, a jolly man in a black top hat, tuck us under a plaid blanket.

The sky was clear, but there was a nip in the air. The park was filled with people jogging, riding bikes, roller-skating, and having picnics on the grass. I'm sure we looked like a normal mother and daughter riding along in our carriage. No one could have guessed we had met for the first time just a couple of hours ago.

"Do I look at all like my father?" I heard myself asking her.

She studied my face for a while. I wasn't sure she was going to answer. "Around the mouth," she said, with some effort. "You have his expression. I noticed that right away. The same way of cocking your head to one side when you talk. And you have his hands."

"I don't like my hands. They're square and pudgy."

"They're nice hands," she said, stroking one for a moment. "And you have his smile. . . . He was full of fun, but he had a serious side too. He wanted to go to medical school. That's why he was working that summer."

"Did he?"

"I don't know."

We rode in silence for a while, watching the driver as he urged the horse to go around two bicycles that had collided.

"What was his name?"

As soon as I asked it, I knew that I shouldn't have. She winced, almost as if I had struck her.

"I haven't spoken his name in all these years."

"I'm sorry."

"Oh, Lori, you must never be sorry with me!" Again she took my hand, and this time she held it against her cheek. "Of course you want to know your father's name. Scott Adams. There, I've said it."

"Scott Adams," I repeated. It didn't sound familiar.

"It's a good American name," she said. "I don't think he was Jewish."

"Then I'm only half Jewish?"

"You're Jewish if your mother is," she replied with emphasis. "I'm not religious, but I feel I am a Jew historically."

That's what Mom always says. It gave me a weird feeling to realize that she and Barbara had something in common.

"I don't know where your father is now," Barbara was saying, "but I can try to find out for you. I have friends who might know what happened to him." Then she added, "It won't be as hard as your finding me."

"I can wait," I said. I knew I wasn't ready to meet my father yet. First I had to get used to knowing her.

Again we rode along in silence. I would have told her about Mom and Dad if she asked. But she still didn't. Maybe she was afraid to. And then, before we knew it, the carriage was back at the starting place, across from Rumpelmayer's, and the driver was helping us out.

"Now you come back again," he told us.

"We will, I promise," Barbara replied.

"I wish he could take me to Penn Station," I said.

"I'll drop you there," she said, hailing a cab. "My car is in a lot in that direction."

The cab was one of those big Checkers with lots of room for your legs. The driver was separated from us by a bulletproof shield—most New York taxis have them now. But the city was looking like a peaceful fairyland as we rolled down Fifth Avenue, past the colorful department store windows and the crowds of weekend strollers.

"Lori's a nice name," Barbara said. "I didn't feel I had a right to give you a name, but you know what I wanted to call you?"

"What?"

"Penny."

"Why Penny?"

"Because you were so little, I guess. I don't know. I just liked it."

When I didn't say anything, she asked, "You're not disappointed in me, are you, Lori?"

"No," I said quickly. "Are you . . . in me?"

"You silly," she replied, grabbing for her handkerchief again. "How could anyone be disappointed in you?"

I didn't know how to say good-bye to her. I sat there clutching my bear and trying to hold back the tears. One dripped down onto the bear's wrapping and made a big wet spot.

"I'll call you, Lori," Barbara said. "I don't know how I'm going to tell my husband. He'll be hurt that I kept such a secret from him."

I nodded. I knew about secrets too.

"But you'll meet him. And your sister too."

We kissed each other politely on the cheek when the cab stopped in front of the station. She held me for a moment, but I didn't hug her back. I couldn't. I kept thinking of Mom and how she wouldn't like it. It would be untrue to her.

I think Barbara understood, because she didn't look cross at all. She gave me a big smile, even though her eyes were filled with tears again.

She wasn't planning to go down to the train track with me, but she did. I waved to her through the window when I found a seat. I watched as the train pulled farther and farther away from her. Until she became a tiny speck in the distance.

twenty-six

I was totally exhausted. There was no one sitting next to me, so I could stretch out. I pulled the paper off the bear and, hugging him tight, I closed my eyes.

I kept thinking about the last act of our play. Emily has died in childbirth and gets permission to go back into the past —back into her childhood. I knew I could really play that scene now. I, too, had visited the land of the dead and relived what had happened long ago. Like Emily, I could see the past while knowing the future, which was the present.

"Do any human beings ever realize life while they live it? —every, every minute?" I whispered to the bear. They were Emily's lines. "That's all human beings are! Just blind people."

I had been as good as blind all these years—willing to accept that I didn't know who gave birth to me. Now I knew. I wasn't blind anymore. I had seen her. Touched the ghostly mysteries of where I came from. I had been born. I belonged on this planet.

I hugged the bear even tighter. I wasn't afraid anymore. Now that I was rooted, nothing could blow me away. I was real.

And yet I was still me.

That was the biggest relief of all.

Still, I wasn't deliriously happy, the way I thought I would be. Because while I understood why Barbara had given me up, I couldn't totally forgive her. She hadn't been strong enough to hold on to me.

Not that I was mad or anything. It was just that there was still some pain down deep inside that wouldn't go away. It made me feel separate from her. She wasn't a stranger—your flesh-and-blood mother could never be that. And she was definitely more than a friend. She was Somebody—there was a connection. But she wasn't family, in the sense that Mom and Dad were. But then again, they weren't really family either. I didn't belong to any of them completely.

A wave of loneliness swept over me. I buried my face in the bear's soft fur so the other passengers wouldn't notice I was sobbing. Why was I crying when I should be so happy that I had met my mother?

The rest of the trip was a blur. I didn't even move when the conductor called out my stop—Southhaven. I heard him, and yet I didn't hear him. As if the place he was calling had nothing to do with me. By the time I realized I was supposed to get off, the train had started up again and was heading on to the next town.

I ran frantically through the cars looking for the conductor. He was taking some tickets up front when I caught up with him.

"Too bad," he commented, looking at his watch. "Next station is two hours up."

"How do I get back to Southhaven from there?" My voice was quavering even though I was trying to stay calm.

He pulled a timetable out of his pocket and scanned its columns. "Let's see, today's Saturday. Not too many trains running. There'll be one coming through Providence 'bout nine o'clock, says here."

I went back to my seat and the bear. If I was lucky I'd get home before Mom and Dad. But, as Dad would say, I couldn't count on it. There were two hours more to go to Providence, and another two hours back. I clutched the bear and snuggled against him, hoping that when I opened my eyes I'd be home in my own bed, instead of still on the train.

The next thing I knew the name "Providence" was ringing through the car. This time I leapt up and ran towards the door. By the time I remembered the bear, the train was pulling away.

But that wasn't the worst of it. The next train back was half an hour late. I didn't get in to Southhaven until midnight. I knew that even with a taxi, my chances of getting home before my folks were slim.

Dad was waiting by the door. He looked relieved to see me, and then he got mad.

"All right, Lori, where have you been?"

"At Maggie's," I said. "Remember, I told you I'd be there."

"Then how do you explain Maggie's mother telling us Maggie went in to New York with Jack and his parents?" When I didn't respond, he went on. "We got home earlier than we expected and called over there right away. Chris hadn't seen you either. And Mrs. O'Brian said that Sue is at a party with Tony. It's time you came clean, young lady. Your mother has been worried sick. We were about to call the police."

I could see Mom in the hall just behind him. She looked awful.

"It's not like you to lie to us," she said.

"Or is it?" snapped my father.

I had been planning to tell them everything eventually, but in a cool way. Not like this. I walked slowly into the den and sat down on the couch. Dad went to his big leather chair, and Mom to hers across from him.

Dad glowered at me, waiting. I had the feeling that if he was the kind of man who beat his children, I would really be getting it. Mom just looked down, letting him take over.

"I've just met my mother," I said.

They were both speechless. They looked at me with horror, as if I'd said the thing they most dreaded to hear.

"What do you mean . . . met your mother?" Mom said at last.

"I met, you know, the woman who gave birth to me."

"How did you do that?" Dad asked, trying to sound like he wasn't about to have a heart attack. Then he went over to the bar and poured himself a drink.

I told them about my history assignment in school and how I wanted to know where I came from—wanted to know my roots. I used almost the same words I used with Barbara, only now it seemed like years ago that I'd been with her in

Rumpelmayer's. I left out the parts about going through Mom's drawers and to the adoption agency. I described the Search and Find meeting, and the stories of the adoptees I'd heard there.

When I got done, we just sat there, almost like strangers, trying to think of something to say to each other. It was as if I was somebody else, and they were somebody else, and we were going to try to be extra polite to each other.

"What did she look like?" Mom asked, trying to sound casual.

"She was pretty," I said, afraid to say too much.

"Did she look like you?"

That's what Mom really wanted to know. Did we look like mother and daughter? Did I feel Barbara was more my mother than she was?

"She's the same height and has the same color hair," I said. "But her eyes are different, and her mouth. I guess I wouldn't have recognized her if I saw her on a bus."

I hadn't even known that until I said it. But it was true. I would not necessarily have picked Barbara out as my mother.

"You should have told us what you were doing," my father said in a tone that was between being angry and hurt.

"I was going to," I replied. "But I wanted to wait until after I'd seen how everything turned out."

"Is she married?" Mom asked.

"Yes."

"And does she have any other children?"

"A four-year-old girl. Her name is Martha. But they call her Muffy." I don't know why I added that detail.

Again we sat there in silence. Dad went out to the kitchen and got some ice for his drink. And made one for Mom without even asking. He knew she needed it. "Would you like a Coke or something, Lori?" he called.

"No thank you."

It was terrible, being so formal with your folks. For a moment I had a feeling of panic—maybe it was all over with us. Maybe what I had done had ended our relationship and we'd never be like we were before. Maybe nothing would ever be the same again.

Only Winkie seemed the same, trotting after Dad, sinking down at his feet in his usual way.

There was another uncomfortable silence. Then Mom spoke in a low voice, as if she was talking to herself, rather than to us.

"You raise a child for sixteen years and you think you know her. You think you're the parents, and then one day you find out that you've been deceiving yourselves."

"What do you mean?" I asked. I was really scared. Even Dad looked sort of startled, as if he was afraid he was about to hear something he didn't want to.

"Just that I was so blind. It never occurred to me that we weren't enough for you. That you were thinking of your mother all this time."

"That's not true," I protested. I felt as if I was fighting for my life. "I wasn't thinking of her *all* the time. Just once in a while. But you told me so many different stories. I couldn't make any sense out of anything. I wanted to know what really happened."

"We didn't know the whole story either," Mom said. "The agency didn't tell us everything. Just what they thought it was important for us to know."

"But you knew my mother's name. It's on my adoption papers."

It was Mom's turn to look startled now. "You saw the adoption papers?"

I nodded yes, but I couldn't look her in the eye.

She wasn't mad. She said, sort of wistfully, "I never really looked at them. I didn't want to know her name. Or anything about her. I wanted to think you were all ours."

"But I am," I said.

She went on as if she hadn't heard me. "I deliberately didn't ask the agency too much about her. Then I wouldn't have to lie if you asked any questions. As long as you were healthy, that's all I cared about. I thought not knowing anything would make us your real parents."

"You are," I continued protesting.

"I never thought that you would *need* to know one day," she said, "that you'd be curious. I was thinking of myself. Not of you." Her voice rose here to a kind of hysterical pitch.

"Maybe we should wait until morning to go into all this," Dad said.

"We've waited too long," Mom countered vehemently. Then, turning to me, she said, "You should have told us about this history assignment, Lori. I've noticed you've been acting very jumpy lately. Moody, I guess is the word. But I dismissed it as something teenagers go through. All the books say that there's a lot of stress in adolescence because of body changes —that teenagers have to experiment in separating from their parents."

"But the books don't know about adopted kids," I said. "We're different. We have four parents, but two are missing. We don't know where they are. It gets very confusing. We feel separate from everyone." I was starting to cry now, but I forced myself to go on. This wasn't a speech in a play. This was for real.

"We feel like freaks," I continued. "We don't know who we look like, who we are. We pretend to be like everyone else, but we know inside that we're not. It's as if we were never born. As if we just floated into the world somehow, but no one will tell us how. All we know is we're adopted." I was really crying by now.

"You don't have to be ashamed of being adopted," my father said awkwardly. He's always at a loss for words when the tears start flowing at our house.

"That's not the point, Harry," Mom said, bursting into tears herself and coming over to me on the couch. We fell into each other's arms. Then Dad came over and started bawling, and we were all hugging and crying together. I'd never seen Dad cry before. Winkie got so alarmed that he leapt up on the couch on top of us. He whimpered so pathetically to be included that we all started laughing and crying at the same time.

I guess we were crying because we'd been afraid of losing each other when we faced the truth. And maybe we weren't really laughing at Winkie, but because we were so relieved that we still cared about each other. We were still the same family.

When we calmed down a little, Mom and Dad asked me

more questions about Barbara. I told them how she hadn't really wanted to give me up, but felt she had no choice. How she had waited a long time to get married and have another child. I sounded like the adult as I spoke, and my folks were the children listening to my story. I was like the mother reassuring them that I wasn't going to leave them for anyone else.

They were as exhausted as I was by now. "Who else is hungry?" Dad said. "I need strength." We went into the kitchen and sat around the table while Mom put out the fried chicken that she had left for me. I even saw her slip a piece to Winkie—something she never allowed any of us to do. She was really in another space.

"You know," she said, "I think we should tell Lori the *real* chosen baby story."

"What do you mean?" Dad asked with his mouth full of food, something he'd always lectured Mike and me about. He was somewhere else too.

"I mean how it was with us when we got her."

"How was it?" he asked, teasing her a little.

"Oh, Harry, you're impossible," she said. She actually blushed. And for that moment I saw Mom as she must have looked when she was younger.

"When Dad and I got married, we never imagined we wouldn't be able to have children of our own," she told me. "I wanted a large family—two boys and two girls. I used to joke with Dad that they should all have my looks, but his brains."

Ordinarily we would have laughed when Mom said something like that. But now Dad didn't look like he felt like laughing. In fact, the corners of his mouth were turned down like they get when he's depressed or worried about something.

"When we found out we couldn't have children, it wasn't easy. We weren't sure how we felt about adoption. We worried that we might not be able to love a child who wasn't our own."

"I'm not sure this story is a good idea, Louise," Dad said.

"*I'm* sure," Mom said firmly, which isn't like her. When Dad speaks strongly about something she usually doesn't argue.

"We talked about it for a long time. Finally we came to the conclusion that we had no choice but to adopt if we wanted to be parents. The social worker at the New York agency kept reassuring us that after a few weeks we wouldn't be able to tell the difference, the child would be so much like us. I made myself believe her."

Dad got up to fix himself another drink. He tripped over Winkie on the way back to the chair. Winkie gave a yelp and crawled under the coffee table.

"It was hard waiting once we'd made the decision. The social worker said she hoped to find a baby who matched our family background and physical characteristics. Every day when I went to work, I would be greeted with: 'Have you got the baby yet?'

"And then one morning I'd no sooner gotten to the office than a call came through that I was to come to the agency with Dad. The switchboard operator contacted him for me, and everyone was congratulating me as I dashed out. There were so many tears of joy streaming down my face, I wasn't sure I was going to be able to drive home to meet Dad. We tore down that highway like speed demons. It's a wonder we weren't killed."

Now there were tears in her eyes again, and I could feel some welling up in mine. Even Dad looked as if he might break down again.

"There wasn't a row of cribs," Mom said. "When Dad and I walked into that small room together, there was just one tiny baby waiting for us—you."

Now the tears came pouring out. "You were so beautiful." Mom gasped. "Oh, Lori, we loved you immediately. That part of the story was always true. You were even more wonderful than we could have imagined."

I think we would have all dissolved in puddles on the floor if the phone hadn't rung just then. Mom pulled herself together and ran for it. A late-night phone call could always mean something with Mike. But it was Mr. O'Brian. He'd seen the lights on downstairs and worried that Mom and Dad were still looking for me.

"She's here and fine," I heard Mom say. "She'd just taken a little excursion. But she came back to us a little while ago."

Mom was smiling again when she rejoined us. "That was really nice of Mr. O'Brian. They're all pretty helpful over there, aren't they?"

I was practically asleep by now, so Mom and Dad told me to go to bed. I kissed them each good night and groped my way up the stairs. I could hear them still talking down below as I fell into a deep sleep.

twenty-seven

  I went over to Sue's the next morning when she and Tony got back from Mass with her dad.

"Oh, Lori, quick, tell us everything!" Sue cried, pulling me into the kitchen for privacy. "I prayed it went well. Did it? I've been so nervous. I couldn't sleep all last night wondering what happened."

"Give her a chance to talk," Tony said, guiding us both to chairs. Then settling himself on a stool next to Sue, he said, "So talk."

And I did. I told them everything. About how I waited outside Rumpelmayer's, and how Barbara looked when she came toward me, and what we didn't eat for lunch, and how she bought the bear for me, and what the horse-and-buggy ride was like. I even described the taxi ride to the station and the horrendous train ride home.

Sue actually had tears in her eyes, but she was smiling all the time.

When I finished telling them how Mom and Dad took it, Tony said, "It was worth all you went through, then?"

"What kind of question is that?" Sue asked him.

"One that any legal team asks its client," he said, taking her hand.

"Yes, it was worth it," I said. And I added, with a laugh, "But I wouldn't want to go through it again."

"And I wouldn't either," said Tony. "But I'm happy for you. In fact, I'm just plain happy. Sue and I have something to tell you."

I knew the minute I looked into their faces what it was. They were absolutely radiant.

"Remember that legal work I did on the marriage certificates?" he asked.

I nodded innocently.

"Well, after Sue and I found Barbara Goldman's, we decided we might just as well go ahead and think about one for ourselves."

"You're going to do it!" I cried, leaping up and hugging them both.

"This summer," Sue said, beaming from ear to ear. "After Tony finishes his exams."

"If they don't finish me first," he said.

"They'd better not," she informed him playfully. "I haven't told you, but this is going to be a modern marriage. You're going to do the shopping, the housework, the dishes and . . ."

"And diaper the baby?" he asked impishly.

That made her blush. "You . . . you leprechaun," she shrieked, shaking his shoulders.

"I've got to get back," I said. "The folks are waiting for lunch." I paused at the door: "And thanks, you guys. You're quite a team."

Mom and Dad were really in a good mood that day, and very yakety. I hadn't seen them that way for a long time.

Dad told me that they'd gotten home early the night before because Mike had clammed up and refused to see them. The doctor felt it was best not to pressure him. They were so depressed that they skipped their card game and came right back. At first it didn't bother them too much that I wasn't at Maggie's, but when it started getting late they were really frantic.

"I was imagining all kinds of horrible things that could have happened to you," Mom said.

"She wanted me to call the police," Dad said. "She was convinced you'd been kidnapped."

"Kidnapped?" I laughed. "Who would want me?"

"I would," Mom said, her eyes shining with love. I thought I was going to cry again.

"I've thought a lot about what you told us last night," she continued. "We're going to try to be open about everything with you from now on. With Mike too." But she added, "If it's possible."

We all sat there quietly thinking about Mike.

"Do you think some of Mike's problems might be related to his adoption?" Mom asked. "Did he ever say anything to you?"

"We never talked about adoption," I said.

But now that she mentioned it, it did seem possible. Boys react differently than girls. I even saw the connection between Mike and Bottomless Pit. Probably both of them had been acting sort of crazy because they had things bottled up inside them. Now that he'd been able to admit things openly, Bottomless Pit seemed changed—except for some wisecracks now and then. Maybe Mike would feel better about himself if he could talk about things he had buried inside.

"Did you ever tell Mike about his real parents?" I asked.

"We didn't learn very much about his background either," Mom said. "I think his mother was only sixteen when she had him."

"My age," I gasped.

"That's right. I don't know how he'd feel about that. I also vaguely remember that his mother was adopted too. It may all be disturbing."

"It's still better to know the truth," I said.

"You may be right," Mom said. "But I don't know how to find out more."

"You could go to the agency where you got him," I suggested. And then I told them about my visit to Ms. Barnes at the Rocking Cradle. They were impressed by that.

"You've been through so much, Lori," Mom said. "And to think we didn't know."

"We would have helped you," Dad said, joining in for the first time. "I would have driven you in to New York myself."

"You would have?" I said in amazement.

"You betcha, Cookie," he replied without hesitation. "If you needed that information, I would have gotten it for you."

Mom wiped her eyes, and Dad blew his nose. I started petting Winkie so I wouldn't cry again.

"We can call that Boston agency about Mike in the morning, Lou," Dad said.

"Don't you think we should talk to Mike's doctor before doing anything?" Mom asked. "I remember his once saying that he didn't want to bring up the subject of adoption until Mike had solved his other problems."

"But that could be a good part of his problem!" I exclaimed.

"I agree with Lori," Dad said. "That doctor may not understand adopted kids."

I couldn't believe it was my dad saying all this.

"I'd still like to discuss it with Mike's doctor," Mom said.

"We can do that too. But in the meantime I'm going to get that information for my son all ready for the day he asks for it."

"My head is spinning," Mom said. "Everything is happening so fast. I don't think I slept all night. There were other things on my mind too. I guess I should tell you."

Dad and I both looked up expectantly.

"I'm going back to work."

Dad seemed more surprised at this than I was.

"I've decided that it's been counterproductive for me to give up the things I really like to do," Mom explained. "I can't tell you how often I've missed getting up and going out to an office. Especially after the kids were at school. But I felt it was my duty to stay home. I might not have been on top of Mike so much if I'd been busy with my own career. I've become just another one of those nagging suburban housewives."

"That's going too far," Dad objected.

"You've been a super mother," I told her. "Kids need mothers home after school waiting for them."

"Well then, I should have gotten a part-time job," she said. "But I'm going back to work now for sure. I think I can be an even better mother for you both if I'm concentrating on more things than the dust in this house."

"What dust?" asked Dad. "I've never seen any dust."

"That's because I've spent all my time protecting you from it," Mom said. "You may find you even like having some around."

"Don't count on it," Dad said.

But even though we all laughed, I think some part of him meant it. Maybe he was used to having Mom available when he needed her too.

I don't want to make it sound as if it was smooth sailing after that. You know, like those fairy tales that tie everything up neatly and say, "They all lived happily ever after."

It wasn't that perfect. For one thing, Mom and Dad looked horrified when I suggested that they meet Barbara.

"I know you'd all get along," I said.

"I don't think I could, just yet," Mom said.

And Dad didn't say anything, which was even worse.

"Give us time," Mom said.

But she didn't say how much.

They must have felt that not meeting Barbara would help make her less real. That if they didn't have to see her, they could almost pretend she didn't exist.

But that wasn't my only concern. I didn't hear from Barbara for about a month after our meeting. And I started to get worried. I thought maybe she hadn't liked me after all. Or didn't want to see me again.

I couldn't say anything to Mom or Dad, but Maggie knew how I was suffering.

"Take the bull by the horns. Call her," Maggie said.

"She's not a bull. And I just can't."

"Why not?"

"She said she'd call me."

"She could have lost your number."

That was a possibility. After all, I'd lost her bear.

I really felt badly about the bear. He was so cute. And he was a present from my mother. Maybe losing him was some terrible omen that I would lose her too.

Just when I couldn't stand it anymore and was going to phone her, she called. Her voice was kind of breathless, like it had been that first time we'd spoken.

"I'm sorry it took me so long to get back to you, Lori," she said.

"Oh, that's okay," I replied, as if I hadn't noticed.

"Can you talk?"

"Yes."

"I was really knocked out after our day together. It stirred up so many things inside me. Things that I had kept repressed for so long."

"Are you all right?"

"I am now. I didn't know so much pain would come out with the happiness. I didn't want to call you while I was feeling that way."

As she was speaking, I remembered Claire's words at the Search and Find meeting—that the one who is found is taken by surprise. I'd been so centered on myself that I hadn't stopped to think how Barbara was feeling about having to deal with the past again. At least I'd had some time to work a lot of things through before calling her.

"I finally got up enough courage to tell my husband just a few days ago," she was saying. "And he's agreed to meet you."

"I'm sorry you've had so much trouble," I said.

"Lori, didn't I tell you not to be sorry? I feel better now, I really do. My husband told me things about his own past that he'd never faced before. It made us kind of closer, talking like that."

"I'm glad."

"But he doesn't think we should tell Muffy until she's a little older. He wants you to meet her as just a friend for now."

"Whatever you say," I replied. But it hurt a little—like I was still the outsider.

"I forgot the bear on the train," I blurted out. I guess I wanted to hurt her a little too.

There was a moment's silence, and then she said, "I worried about that afterward. I shouldn't have asked you to take it. You're not a baby anymore—you're a lovely young woman. We have to see each other as we are now—not as we were."

"I know what you mean," I said.

"Have you told your parents?" she asked.

"Yes."

"What did they say? I hope they weren't angry with me."

"Why should they be? I called you."

"They didn't mind?"

"They understood."

"I'd like to meet them. To thank them for raising such a wonderful girl."

"Someday," was all I could say.

"Another thing," she went on. "I don't know quite how to put this. But I managed to find out where your father is. He lives on the West Coast. It was difficult for me. But I called him—last night."

There was another silence on the line. For a minute I thought we'd been disconnected.

"Hello?" I said.

"Hello, I'm still here. He was really surprised to hear from me. And embarrassed. You can imagine." This last with a little laugh. "He said he has a wife and two young daughters now. He wants to let it all sink in for a while." She gave another nervous laugh. "He hasn't changed much."

"It's okay," I said. "I don't care."

That was true, in a way. I mean, it was Barbara who carried me for nine months and had to make arrangements for my life.

While she was going on about how many people she'd had to call to learn my father's whereabouts, I thought of some of Mr. Innskeep's favorite lines of Shakespeare:

> Full fathom five thy father lies;
>   Of his bones are coral made:
> Those are pearls that were his eyes;
>   Nothing of him that doth fade,
> But doth suffer a sea-change
> Into something rich and strange.

The idea of a father out there was still something rich and strange to me. But I wasn't ready for him any more than he was for me. I had to leave it buried—full fathom five. For now.

"I'd like to see you again . . . when you have time," Barbara said hesitantly. "How is school going?"

"I'm busy with the play and my history report," I said.

(Actually, I'd really neglected the report. I still had another book on child welfare to read by the next week.)

"Do you want to wait until school is over? We could get together during the summer."

"Sure," I said. "I'll call you when I get out."

I couldn't believe my words. All my life I'd wanted to meet my mother, and now that I had, I was casually agreeing to wait until some indefinite date to see her again. But there really wasn't any hurry anymore. Knowing about myself was what mattered most. There were years ahead for us to get to know each other.

Also, in spite of their trying to understand, I knew Mom and Dad would be hurt if I saw Barbara too much. Mom kept saying she was happy for me. But she still didn't seem in any hurry to meet Barbara. And Dad never mentioned her anymore. It was a subject no one brought up. I guess they needed time to absorb everything too. You could tell that Dad wanted to act as if nothing had happened, that I was still his Cookie and we'd all go on as before. Which we would—in a way.

Nothing is ever exactly the same. Mr. Innskeep once said you can never step in the same river twice. He was quoting some Greek philosopher. And he was right.

twenty-eight

Where was Chris during all this? Out with René Welles, the prettiest girl in the senior class. It was rumored that he'd asked her to the senior prom. When I passed them in the halls, I'd turn away as if I didn't see them holding hands.

"It's worth it to lose Chris to gain my mother," I told Maggie as we were cleaning out our gym lockers.

"What profit a man if he gain the world and lose his soul?" Maggie said, unknotting a shoelace. And then, as if horrified by what she'd quoted, she said, "I mean, what profit a *person.*"

She had been influenced by Lisa's mania for changing sexist words like mankind to humankind, chairman to chairperson, and so on. "Someone should do a feminist annotation of Shakespeare," Maggie said. "I'll take it up with Mr. Innskeep."

"Stick to the point, Maggie," I said impatiently, not wanting the subject to be changed from Chris to Shakespeare.

"What was the point?"

"That it's better to gain a mother and lose a disloyal *person.*"

"You haven't lost him," she said. And when I didn't answer, she added, "But you have lost your heart."

"Corny," I said, jamming my dirty gym stuff into my bookbag, even though I knew it wouldn't all fit.

"It's not serious with René," Maggie went on. "He's on the rebound. Jack says he's still wild about you."

"I don't want to talk about him," I said. "I've got to keep my mind on my report for tomorrow. I'm so sick of orphans, they're coming out of my ears."

"You're going to go through with the orphan bit?" Maggie asked casually.

"I've gone this far, I might as well. There's no point blowing my cover now. Anyway, Mr. Innskeep lent me all those books on child welfare. He's all psyched to hear about it."

I didn't know whether I was trying to convince her, or myself. I just knew I had never considered changing the subject of my report.

"Yeah, I guess you're right," Maggie said. "And what's your conclusions after all your reading?"

"The history of childhood is totally grim," I told her. "Centuries ago people used to drown unwanted babies like kittens. Or they'd poison them, strangle them, or leave them on some mountain to die. That was in the days before there were orphanages—and orphanages were no picnic either. Should I go on?"

"Save the punchlines for tomorrow," she said, flipping her things into Lisa's antinuke tote bag. "I'll be there with a cheering squad."

"I'll need one," I said.

There was a thick forest of family trees on Mr. Innskeep's walls when we filed into his classroom the next day. And his desk was piled high with the excavations of his family explorers. I was the last one to present my material.

I wasn't even nervous when Mr. Innskeep called my name. There was nothing personal in what I had written and I like to read aloud. All I had to do was stick to the important points I'd underlined, and ad lib here and there.

"My paper is called 'Physical and Spiritual Orphans'," I told the class. "I'll start from the present and work my way back through history." And then I went on to explain: "Orphans are not usually orphans as we think of them. Very few people are really orphans, because how could both of your parents just happen to die? There aren't that many earthquakes or plane crashes or outbreaks of bubonic plague."

This got a few appreciative guffaws.

"Most of the children we call orphans have one living parent," I continued. "But usually that parent can't take care of them for some reason—illness or poverty. And so the kid ends up in a foster care home or an orphanage. Such kids are very sad, and sometimes they must dream of how wonderful it would be to be adopted by a family who would love them and take care of them."

And then I heard myself talking about adoption. I hadn't planned to. It wasn't in my paper. But once I had mentioned it, I couldn't get off the point.

"Most adopted kids weren't orphans to begin with. They usually had living parents who couldn't keep them because they weren't married or were too poor. But they feel like orphans because no one has ever told them the truth about who they come from. They feel sad and lonely even though they get a lot of love. There's an empty space inside them that nothing can fill."

I went on and on like that, not even pretending to look at my paper now. It was just flowing out of me, as if this was what I was supposed to be talking about.

"Lori, this is fascinating," Mr. Innskeep said when I stopped at one point to take a deep breath. It was like I was coming up from underwater gulping for air. "Your report has psychological depth. Did you find these ideas about adoption in those child welfare books?"

"I didn't need any books," I said, looking right at him. "I lived it. I'm adopted."

There was a kind of gasp that went through the room. You would have thought I'd announced I was from Krypton or somewhere else in outer space.

"Is your report on adoption, then?" Mr. Innskeep asked, trying to sound as unruffled as possible.

"It's on *my* adoption," I heard myself saying. "I'm not ashamed to talk about it anymore. I've been a coward until now. And that's what I should be ashamed of. Right from the beginning I should have said I'd speak on what it's like to be adopted. How it feels when your records are sealed and you have no right to know who you are. How you have the need to go out and search for your real parents, to find out who they are and why they gave you up."

"Did you do that?" Mr. Innskeep asked. He didn't seem at all upset that I was changing my story about my parents being orphans.

"Yes," I replied. "I beat the system, in a way, by getting around the sealed records. I found my mother even though I wasn't supposed to."

"Would you like to tell us what it was like for you? You don't have to." Mr. Innskeep was obviously torn between being considerate and being curious.

"I don't mind," I said. "Everyone else has said things that were difficult for them. Why shouldn't I?"

And then I went on to try to describe my feelings during my search. "I was really scared a lot of the time," I admitted. "I went through different periods of feeling happy, sad, guilty, alone, and even mad. And I cried a lot during each one—even the happy ones. But it was worth it, because now I know the truth about where I came from and why my mother had to give me up."

No one said anything. It was like I was spinning out a mystery thriller the way they sat there waiting for me to continue.

"My mother felt she didn't have a choice," I said. "In those days it was hard for girls to keep their babies when they weren't married. Everyone said it was better for the baby to be put up for adoption. She thought she was doing the best thing for me."

"Did you meet your father too?" Mr. Innskeep asked.

"Not yet. But I will." And even as I said it, I knew that someday I would.

Then I went back to my desk and pulled out two sheets, each one with an empty family tree.

"I haven't had the courage to fill in either one yet," I confessed. "But I'm ready to now. Both of them."

"You don't have to, Lori," Mr. Innskeep said quickly. "I'll give you a grade without them."

"But I want to," I insisted. "Not for your class, but for myself. I should know what's on both of these trees, because they both belong to me. In different ways. It's not only for myself. Someday my kids may want to know."

I was amazed to hear myself add that last part—about kids. It just came out.

And then I noticed for the first time that Chris was sitting in the back of the class. He must have been blocked from view before. I blushed purple (I'm sure) and sat down.

Stephanie was waving her hand in the air.

"Do you have a question?" Mr. Innskeep asked. He always opened discussion to the class after a report.

"Yes. This is *totally* fascinating. And I'm curious about how Lori's adoptive parents feel about it."

"They understand," I said from my desk. "It's not exactly easy for them, but they're glad I told them. We're more relaxed with each other now that there are no more secrets."

"Do you look like your mother?" Hortense asked.

"A little. But not so much."

"Would you advise other adopted kids to search?" Artie asked.

I had to think about that for a minute. "Okay, only if they're ready for shocks," I said, feeling like Claire now. "After they've thought about it really hard. Because your mother may not be ready for you when you find her. Especially if she's been keeping it all a secret. It might take her time to come around. You have to understand that, and not think she's rejecting you."

"But do you think it's *better* for adopted kids to search for their real parents?" Whitney asked.

"I think everyone has a right to know who gave birth to them," I said. "And once you know, I guess you'd really want to meet that person. It's only natural."

"But I'm still not sure it's totally fair to the adoptive parents who raised you," Stephanie broke in. "What do you think, Jeffrey?"

It was hard to tell if Bottomless Pit looked startled because he'd been asked to give an opinion, or because Stephanie had called him Jeffrey rather than his nickname. He flushed, but then he stood up awkwardly.

"I'll have to think about it," he said. "I'm not ready to give an answer yet." And he sat down.

Mr. Innskeep took over here. "The point to remember is that Lori did what she felt she had to do. We all have different needs at various stages of our lives." And then, quoting Polonius's advice to Hamlet, which he loved to do, he added, " 'This above all: to thine own self be true . . . Thou canst not then be false to any man.' "

After class the kids gathered around me, wanting to know how I'd found my mother, what she looked like, and everything. I saw Bottomless Pit hovering nearby taking it all in, but he didn't come over.

Maggie was waiting with Chris outside the door.

"Hi," he said sheepishly.

"What are you doing here?" I asked huffily.

"Maggie invited me," he said with a sly smile. "I came as her guest."

"Maggie, how could you?" I cried.

"Come off it, Lori," Maggie said. "I thought it would be a good excuse to get you two together again. Your report was supposed to be on orphans. And Chris has been looking like an orphan since you two broke up."

"Some orphan," I said. "He seems to have found someone to take care of him."

"That was only foster care," Chris broke in. "I want to be *adopted* by you, Lor."

He looked so cute when he said it that I smiled in spite of myself.

"How about a Coke at the Fiery Ox to make it legal?" he added quickly.

I looked at Maggie helplessly. "Will you come too?"

"Now, you don't need your ma at a time like this, child," he drawled. "Your ma has other fish to fry now."

And when I just stood there, she prodded me. "You two just run along, hear!"

The Fiery Ox was almost deserted, as usual. I hadn't been here since that time we'd had the fight. Someone was hanging over the jukebox, which was blaring out country rock. I couldn't hear the lyrics, just the whine of longing in the singer's voice.

"I got into Colorado State," Chris said as soon as we sat down.

"That's great," I said, though I had already heard it from Maggie.

"You can come out to visit. I'll teach you how to ski."

"If Mom and Dad will let me."

"Tell them I'll be the chaperone."

"Then I'll never get to come."

He put his arm around me. I realized how much I'd missed him.

"I've got a secret to tell too, Lor. You're not the only one who's been hiding things."

I remembered he had sort of hinted at this when he'd come back from spring vacation.

"Don't tell me you're adopted," I said half jokingly.

"Adopted people aren't the only ones who feel lost," he said. "Everyone feels disconnected in some way, even when they know who their parents are. You know that line in the Kurt Weill song, 'We're all of us lost in the stars'? Well, we are. We're all lost in the mystery of this universe. We don't know how we got here, or why."

He sounded like a poet, a sad one, who had glimpsed some terrible truth.

"What were you going to tell me?" I asked, almost afraid to hear.

"About my brother—Eddie."

When he didn't go on, I said, "What about him?"

"He was a great guy. He had everything—looks, talent, personality. He could charm a bird off a tree."

"He could?" I noticed we were using the past tense. "Where's he now?"

It was like he hadn't heard me.

"He wanted to be a painter. But my old man insisted he go into real estate with him. Eddie tried, but he just couldn't hack being a salesman. 'Selling God's green earth instead of putting it on canvas'—that's the way he saw it."

"And what happened?"

"He just copped out. Took drugs. Anything he could lay his hands on."

Again Chris stopped talking and sat there staring into space.

"Where is he now?" I asked softly.

"Dead."

"Oh, no."

"He committed suicide."

I was really shocked.

"The papers ran it as a car crash. You know, car hits pole head-on. Driver killed. But I knew he had been overdosing. He meant to do it. He wanted to get away—somehow."

"How'd your parents take it?"

"They fell apart. Dad started drinking. They fought all the time. I started taking drugs. They split up. I got kicked out of two schools. They shipped me off here to Mom's sister. It was like my last chance."

"You mean they didn't take that round-the-world trip?"

"No way."

The vein in Chris's forehead was throbbing now, like it does when he gets intense about something.

"I felt so guilty," he said. "Me alive, Eddie dead. If I'd been more alert, I could have stopped him. I should have known he was trying to destroy himself."

"No one can save someone else if they don't want to be saved," I said, holding on to his hand real tight.

"I should have done something," Chris insisted.

"There's nothing you could have done. Don't torture yourself. You can't rewrite history."

We sat in silence for a while.

"But there's some good news too," he said. "My parents got together again just before I went home."

"That's wonderful," I exclaimed, squeezing his hand.

"They'd been hinting in their letters. And when I arrived, Dad was back in the house."

"I wish you'd told me all this before," I said. "It would have helped."

"I couldn't at first," he said. "And then when I was going to —after vacation—you seemed so changed."

"I thought you didn't understand me. There I was going to meet my real mother for the first time, and all you could think about was my adopted parents."

"I guess I knew how fragile families are. They seem so solid and then suddenly—pow—they're gone. You have those great parents, and I was afraid you were going to blow it."

"You mean, you wanted to save me."

He nodded. His eyes were getting sort of teary, like mine.

"Oh, Chris, you're wonderful!" I brought his hand up to my lips and held it there.

"Did anyone ever tell you you have a funny face?" he said, nipping my nose with his teeth. "But at least it will be dark at the senior prom."

And then we ordered king-sized hamburgers and milk shakes. Anyone watching us gobble them down would have thought we hadn't a care in the world.

twenty-nine

Mike came home from the hospital in time to see the play. He was much calmer. I won't say he wasn't still bratty in lots of ways, but it was a relief to have him back in any form.

"The doctor talked with Mike about adoption for a few sessions," Mom told me. "He said Mike seemed a little curious about who his parents were, but he also seemed full of anger. He just wasn't ready to deal with it yet."

"Did the doctor tell him about my search?"

"No, he didn't feel that he should," Mom said. "He thought you should tell Mike yourself—when you were ready."

And so Mike and I didn't talk directly about what either of us had been through. But we had our ways.

"How's the dungeon, Flug?" I asked him that first night he was home. "Slay any demons or dragons?"

"Lots of them," he said. He was sitting on his bed, his suitcases half unpacked. "But a few of them knocked me out, too."

"But you opened some doors?" I asked.

"Yeah, doors I hadn't known about before."

"And you overpowered the demons there?"

"Most of them," he replied. "There are one or two left to do."

"There's time," I said. "You can't open all the doors at once."

"I wouldn't want to."

"I opened some doors, too, Flug."

"I figured you were up to something."

"It wasn't easy. I'll tell you about it sometime."

He looked up at me curiously.

"It's good to have you back, Flug," I said. "I missed you."

"I asked to come back specially to see your play," Mike said, almost shyly. "I can stay if . . . if I can keep my cool."

"You will," I said. "A Dungeon Master can do anything."

I noticed that his voice had gotten a little gravelly, as if it was getting ready to change. And there was some dark fuzz on his upper lip. My little brother was growing up.

Bottomless Pit came up to me the day before the play and asked if I was nervous. He said he remembered how jittery he was when he played Sitting Bull.

"I'm always scared when I go onstage," I admitted. "It's those first few minutes that are the hardest."

"Yeah, it's hard to begin anything," he said. I thought he was going to walk on, but he paused and added, "I liked your report the other day."

"You did?" I was really surprised, because I was sure he must have hated it. I was worried that it made him feel foolish since he'd been running around locating all kinds of adopted relatives for his family tree, while I had gone out and gotten the real thing.

"I may begin poking around myself one of these days," he said.

"Don't do it until you're prepared for shocks," I warned.

"Were you prepared?"

"I guess not fully," I said. "How can anyone be *full* prepared?"

"I told my parents about you last night," he said. "They admitted that it could have been a false rumor that the hospital with all my records burned down."

"You're on your way, then," I said. "Once you start there's no turning back. That's one thing I learned."

"Sitting Bull never turns back," he said. And then, giving a war whoop, he ran off down the hall. He was still the same ol Bottomless Pit.

I expected to be a nervous wreck the night of the play—and I was. Fortunately, Dad said he'd drive me to school an hour early, but unfortunately, I kept forgetting things and had to keep running back into the house. Once I tripped over Winkie and almost fell.

"Break a leg," Mom said. I guess that expression's been around a long time.

"At this rate I'll break them both," I said.

"Don't count on it," quipped Mike.

Miss Lathem helped us with our makeup. Maggie looked great with white hair. You could really believe she was my mother. I wore an old-fashioned gingham dress that Miss Lathem had found in a flea market. For the first scene, when I was still a little girl, I put my hair in braids. Jack was prancing about in knickers and a white sailor shirt.

"Break a leg," we kept shouting to each other.

When we all got bored admiring ourselves, Maggie and I sneaked onstage to peek through the curtain. The auditorium was packed tight with relatives and friends. There were even people standing in the back.

I saw Mom and Dad and Mike sitting in the third row center. Lisa and Alan were just behind them. And Maggie's grandparents were in the front row seats Maggie had reserved for them. They'd said they wouldn't miss seeing her for the world.

Mr. Innskeep was sitting towards the back between a man and a woman. But we couldn't tell if he was with one or both of them. Bottomless Pit was sitting far right with his parents and some of the kids from the class. Sue and Tony were far left. Jack's father was busy autographing his new book, *Exploring the Root Canal,* in the aisle nearby.

I wanted to wave to Chris, who was sitting in the second row. We were going out to celebrate with Maggie and Jack after the performance. But just as I was getting ready to stick my arm out, Miss Lathem appeared and pulled us away from the curtain.

"I'm surprised at you girls," she said. "That's not professional."

Standing in the wings, waiting for the curtain to go up, I got butterflies in my stomach again. I was sure I'd forget my lines. I'd just walk out there and draw a complete blank. And that wouldn't be professional either. . . .

It almost happened. I could hardly get my first few lines out, let alone *modulate* and *project*.

But I picked up steam as the first act moved along.

I was really hitting my stride by the time Maggie said, "Emily, come and help me string these beans for the winter." And I had the audience eating out of my hand when I tilted my head and asked coyly:

"Mama, am I good looking?"

ABOUT THE AUTHOR

BETTY JEAN LIFTON, playwright, journalist, and author, has drawn from her own experiences and those that hundreds of other adoptees have shared with her to write her first novel, *I'm Still Me*. She is also the author of *Twice Born: Memoirs of an Adopted Daughter* and *Lost and Found: The Adoption Experience*. Her many stories for children and two highly praised nonfiction books, *A Place Called Hiroshima* and *Children of Vietnam* (with Thomas C. Fox), reflect her years of living in the Far East. Her articles have appeared in numerous magazines, including *The New York Times Magazine, Saturday Review,* and *Seventeen*. She lives in New York City with her husband, Robert Jay Lifton, and a menagerie of assorted pets left behind when her son and daughter left for college.

STEP ON A CRACK

Fifteen-year-old Sarah loves her mother, so why does she dream of murdering her?

When Sarah's eccentric Aunt Kat comes to visit, the terrible nightmares that have bothered Sarah for years become worse and worse until Sarah feels herself losing control. That's when her best friend Josie steps in and together the two girls struggle to uncover the tormenting secret locked deep within Sarah's past.

"Suspenseful ... The author succeeds in creating an atmosphere of mystery and terror which impels the reader to finish the book at a single sitting."—*Hornbook*

Buy STEP ON A CRACK by Mary Anderson, author of *The Rise and Fall of a Teen-age Wacko* wherever Bantam Books are sold or use this handy coupon for ordering.